THE WAREHOUSE INDUSTRY

The Warehouse Industry

William Macbeth

THISTLE
PUBLISHING

All Rights Reserved

Copyright © William Macbeth 2017

This first edition published in 2017 by:

Thistle Publishing
36 Great Smith Street
London
SW1P 3BU

www.thistlepublishing.co.uk

'The dream of death is only the dark smoke
 Under which the fires of life are burning.'

Hermann Hesse, *The Wanderer*

Prologue

A New Beginning

It was a fine spring afternoon. I walked round the back of a nondescript building in a nondescript industrial estate in a wholly unremarkable town, and there I found the manager, scowling and drinking a cup of what I imagined was tea. In those days when you saw someone drinking a cup of something, it was usually tea.

"Have you got any jobs?" I asked him. I had heard or read somewhere that he did have jobs, and I needed one. Otherwise, I would not have asked him if he had any. I would have been doing something else.

The manager looked at me as if he suspected me of some foulness, but said nothing.

"I'm looking for a job," I said. "Have you got any jobs?" I asked again. I needed a job. I didn't particularly want one, but I needed one.

You just can't get by without a job. It's one of those things.

"OK. What can you do?" he said, gruffly. At least I'm pretty sure he said it gruffly.

"Um," I said. I didn't really know what to say. "I can lift and, um, carry things." I was struggling. The manager looked at me disgustedly. He didn't look too impressed; in fact, he looked distinctly unimpressed. "I can remember things," I continued hopefully. It was, if not a remarkable skill, at least a necessary one.

It was the warehouse industry that, for some reason, I wished to work in.

The manager finished his cup of tea with a noisy gulp and a satisfied exhalation, but he didn't offer me one - a cup of tea, I mean. Instead he gave me what I remember as a searching look, as if he was trying to figure something out. Perhaps it was me he was trying to figure out.

"OK, I'll give you a go," he said. He must have been desperate. "You start now," he continued. It was an order. Pretty much everything the manager ever said was an order of some sort; or at least pretty much everything he said to me was an order of some sort.

"Follow me," said the manager.

He placed his empty mug on a desk and casually issued some instructions to someone standing vacantly nearby, before walking briskly through a door. I followed him because that was what he told me to do.

The manager was going to give me a go. It was the best I could have hoped for.

Part One

The Pie Factory

I worked in a pie factory once. I had heard that they weren't too fussy and didn't ask too many questions. At the time I was trying not to draw attention to myself, and so working at the pie factory seemed like a good idea.

I was living with a girl I used to live with at the time: the girl I used to live with when I worked at the pie factory. Working at the pie factory was her idea.

"You should get a job," she told me once. "The pie factory is always looking."

I met her at the pub she worked at and once, at her behest, tried unsuccessfully to have sex with her behind a skip in the car park. The attempt was unsuccessful because after a few awkward thrusts my knees began to hurt unbearably and I had to stop.

She rashly asked me to move in with her after only knowing me for a week or two. I have no idea why. It was a rash act, which she would soon regret.

I've never understood how people can say they don't have any regrets. That doesn't make any sense to me. I have loads of regrets; I regret virtually everything.

My time at the pie factory lives on in my memory in the form of one of those documentaries from the past about the ordinary working lives of ordinary working people. I see burly men with bare chests and scarred, haggard faces shovelling coal; I see robust women working in rows with grim, inhuman efficiency; and I see greasy teenagers who look as if they wish they were dead or had never been born at all.

How I fit into this scene isn't exactly clear. I imagine that I wander through it like a ghost; like a ghost in a pie factory.

My job was to monitor the pie-filling machine. The pie-filling machine was the machine that filled the pies. It was an important machine because without it the pies would be empty, and it needed to be monitored. Sometimes even machines make mistakes.

The pies marched incessantly, day after day, from a large steel container along a conveyer belt into another even larger steel container, which seemed, mysteriously, to operate on multiple levels and juddered as it did whatever it was doing to the pies that disappeared inside.

I imagined that all sorts of terrible, unspeakable things happened to the pies inside the even larger steel container.

Sometimes I imagined the pies were people. Sometimes I gave them names like John or Jane, and attributed to them personality traits like avarice or bravery that a pie couldn't possibly possess; and I deplored John's avarice and I admired Jane's bravery. I did these things because monitoring the pie-filling machine was almost unimaginably dull, as I'm sure you can imagine.

Sometimes the pies came out crooked and that was where I came in, swooping in to scoop out the crooked pie from its hollow and fling it swiftly into a bin by my side, which during the day gradually filled with crooked pies until it needed to be emptied, which was also where I came in.

There were several others who worked on the pie-filling machine performing various functions, none of which made much sense to me.

By mid-morning we were all invariably in a state of pie-induced hypnosis. No one spoke. No one smiled.

Swoop, scoop, fling.
Swoop, scoop, fling.
Swoop. Scoop. Fling.
Empty the bin.
That was how my day would go.

Then the bell would ring for lunch. Or at least that's what happens in the documentary film. I'm not sure if the pie factory actually had a bell. It probably didn't, to tell the truth. But let's just say that the bell would ring. You can imagine it ringing if you like.

"Riiinnngggggg," said the bell.
"Rrrriiinnnngggggggg."
"Rrrrrriiiiinnnnnnggggggggggggg."

The lunch break, which occurred each day at exactly the same time, depressed me. It depressed me partly because it occurred each day at exactly the same time, and partly because after spending all morning looking at pies, I didn't really feel too inclined to eat one. Nevertheless, I ate. But without relish.

Even though it was a break from monitoring the pie-filling machine, I found lunch depressing as it reminded me how I spent my days: monitoring the pie-filling machine and eating lunch.

It was the third or fourth day that I had worked at the pie factory, and I was enduring a particularly bleak lunch break. The crust of the pie I was eating stuck in my throat; the filling of the pie I was eating made me feel sick and reminded me that part of how I spent my days was eating lunch, which depressed me.

I was sitting alone at a table when a man came and sat opposite me. I didn't look up, but I could sense that he was scrutinising me.

"Do I know you?" he said, eventually, in a voice that was low and raw. I looked up.

We had never spoken, but he probably did recognise me, as I recognised him, from a house we both used to go to to buy weed.

"Yeah, I think you might," I answered vaguely, because I didn't really have a choice. I wished that he would leave me alone to bask in my misery, but he wasn't going to.

"I thought so. Do you want a bomb?" he said, casually, as if he was asking me to pass the tomato sauce.

I nodded, and within seconds he had pressed a sweaty ball of cigarette paper into my opened palm with such exaggerated discreetness that it wasn't really discreet at all.

I popped it into my mouth and swallowed. In those days, if someone offered me something I usually just took it without asking too many questions.

I have never been one for making a fuss.

"Thanks," I said. I might have tried to sound grateful but, if I did, I very much doubt that I was successful.

"No worries," said the man. He placed another bomb carefully on his tongue and washed it down with the dregs of the drink he was drinking. "Certainly makes this fucking place more bearable." He laughed, grimly.

I tried to laugh too, but I didn't have too much success.

We continued eating in silence.

If you work in a pie factory I definitely wouldn't recommend taking speed during a shift. It doesn't help. It only magnifies the tedium of spending time at the pie factory. It only makes the seconds sluggish and the minutes interminable. I experienced no pie-nirvana, pie-euphoria or pie-ecstasy. Only tedium. Seemingly endless, almost unbearable tedium: pie-tedium.

I don't remember leaving work that day, but I definitely did. You don't need to remember everything.

After leaving work, I walked until I came to the old derelict stadium, which was situated on the outskirts of town and which, for some reason, reminded me of the past. When I got there, I squeezed between a rusty old fence that had long ago given up guarding the old derelict stadium, or doing anything useful whatsoever, and walked towards an old turnstile that reminded me of the past. Next to the old turnstile that reminded me of the past were some old concrete steps that reminded me of the past and led to what can only be described as an old concrete dungeon, which, for some reason, also reminded me of the past.

The old concrete dungeon might once have been used for something, but was no longer used for anything at all. I'd been there before; I'd played there as a child. Maybe that was why it reminded me of the past.

I walked down the old concrete steps and sat down on the floor of the old concrete dungeon. I sat with my head resting on my knees. It was dark. I sat in the darkness.

I tried not to think about anything, which is harder than it sounds, but which I was able to do without too much trouble.

Some hours later, when the moon had risen and was full and bright overhead, its light pouring through the opening of the old concrete dungeon, I lifted my head. The moonlight reminded me of the past. I stood up and ascended the steps.

I felt an odd sense of freedom as I emerged into the still moonlit night, as if something had changed.

But nothing had changed.

It was an odd sense of freedom. It was a sort of freedom, but not really like freedom at all.

It was a strange feeling and reminded me of the past.

Leaving the Pie Factory

I didn't last long at the pie factory. I didn't last long anywhere to tell the truth. I think, perhaps, I was worried that if I stayed anywhere too long I might start to draw attention to myself and, as I have mentioned, I was trying not to draw attention to myself.

So, I left quietly without telling anyone, so as not to draw attention to myself.

I also left the girl I used to live with when I worked at the pie factory quietly without telling anyone. I didn't even tell the girl I used to live with when I worked at the pie factory herself. There didn't seem any point; she would find out soon enough. First, she would realise that I wasn't there, and then she would realise that I wasn't coming back, and then she would realise that I had left quietly without telling anyone.

I stole hundreds of pounds from her before I left. She always kept hundreds of pounds in a drawer by her bed, in case of emergency she used to say, although I'm not sure what kind of emergency would require hundreds of pounds in a drawer. It was a great temptation, and I've always thought that people can't really be blamed for giving in to temptation. It's to be expected. It's what people are designed to do, and it takes a special effort not to. And people can't really be blamed for not making a special effort, can they? They can be blamed for making no effort at all, but not for not making a special effort.

I didn't blame myself for stealing her money; I decided that I was wholly blameless. If anything, I decided, she only had herself to blame. She really should have known better.

Soon after leaving the pie factory and the girl I used to live with when I worked at the pie factory, I also left the town where I had lived all my life. I left quietly without telling anyone.

I didn't tell anyone I was leaving. Not even mother.

I used some of the money I had stolen to buy a ticket for a bus that would take me to another town where no one knew who I was, and I would be better able to not draw attention to myself.

I boarded the bus and sat in a cushioned seat. I imagined the girl I used to live with when I worked at the pie factory telling her friends what had happened; I imagined her friends telling her that it was for the best, and that she was better off without me.

"It's for the best," one of her friends would say. "You're better off without him."

"After all," another would continue, "what kind of loser works in a pie factory?"

And the girl I used to live with when I worked at the pie factory would say, "Yeah, I suppose you're right. I just wish he'd told me he was going. And I just wish he hadn't stolen hundreds of my pounds."

And I knew I couldn't really blame her if she didn't regret my leaving at all. I knew I only had myself to blame.

Cheap Pillow Mountain

One day there was a delivery of hundreds of cheap pillows. I remember the day – the day hundreds of cheap pillows were delivered – like this: I am standing in the warehouse and hundreds of cheap pillows have been dumped on the floor, like a cheap cloud that has fallen to earth.

It took me a long time to unload the cheap pillows from the back of the lorry that transported them, and all the while the manager watched me suspiciously, as if he suspected that the moment he looked away I would stop unloading the cheap pillows, or would run off with as many cheap pillows as I could carry. He didn't help; he just watched me suspiciously and smoked aggressively, as if he hated the cigarette he was smoking almost as much as he hated me.

There were moments when I was unloading the cheap pillows when it seemed as though there were an infinite number of cheap pillows, as if all the cheap pillows in the world had been magically packed into the back of the lorry. There were moments when I thought I would be unloading cheap pillows for the rest of my life. But, sure enough, eventually, I finished unloading the cheap pillows.

The hundreds of cheap pillows, being impossible to stack efficiently, formed a cheap pillow mountain wedged between two aisles of storage units. It was quite a spectacular sight for cheap pillows.

The manager looked pleased. It was an impressive purchase, his expression seemed to suggest, though I've never been too much of an expert when it comes to reading people's expressions. "Count them," he said. "Make sure they're all there. I'll be back later to see how you're getting on." And then he rushed off up the stairs to his office to go and do something else. I guess he had better things to do than watch me count cheap pillows.

The mountain of cheap pillows reminded me of being a child in my parents' garage at home, which was full of all the junk that people acquire during a lifetime that they don't want to throw away or use.

Left to myself, I decided to scale the heights of the cheap pillow mountain, which in the circumstances seemed like a perfectly reasonable thing to do.

I giggled to myself as I scrambled and clambered up the slope of the cheap pillow mountain, as cheap pillows gave way beneath me; I smiled with glee as I approached the peak of the cheap pillow mountain. Cheap pillows shifted around me. Slowly I began to sink; soon I was engulfed. The cheap pillows were luminous and smelt like brand new things. I felt like an explorer in an unknown territory that no one else was interested in.

I didn't move; I had surrendered, surrounded by the luminous cheap pillows, which were like clouds waiting for their opportunity to float across the sky.

I probably could have stayed there all day but the manager disturbed my bliss. He probably wanted to check that I was doing what I was told. But I hadn't done what I was told. Instead, I had climbed to the peak of the cheap pillow mountain. I had surrendered myself to the smell of brand new things and to memories of the past, and I knew that there was no way he could possibly understand.

I could hear him stomping around the perimeter of the cheap pillow mountain. "Where is that fucking cunt?" he said under his breath, but loud enough for me to hear. He stomped around. He soon gave up. He was never going to spend too long looking for me, and to tell the truth there weren't too many places to look. "For fuck's sake," he said, his heavy footsteps retreating. "Where the fuck is he?"

Once disturbed, I couldn't recapture the thrill of being entirely surrounded by the cheap cloudlike pillows. It suddenly seemed like a tawdry thing to be surrounded by so many cheap pillows. Not without difficulty, I crawled out once I heard the manager's heavy footsteps retreating.

I spent the rest of the morning checking the order to avoid being reprimanded by the manager. I would do most things to avoid being reprimanded by the manager. Being reprimanded by the manager was more disagreeable than doing most things.

I counted the pillows slowly, without enthusiasm, and dismantled the cheap pillow mountain in a listless daze. The destructive results of my labour depressed me.

By lunchtime I was so overcome by lethargy I could barely muster the energy to move. The cheap pillow mountain was gone, and the pillows had been counted and stored as efficiently as possible, which wasn't too efficiently, but my labour had left me feeling dispirited. I needed to go home; I didn't feel too great. The thought of doing even one more thing before I left filled me with horror and despair.

I went upstairs and knocked on the door of the manager's office.

The manager had a daughter – the manager's daughter – who, for some reason, seemed to like me. The manager's daughter worked for her father doing something that I was never able to fathom. She worked at a desk just outside her father's office and she smiled at me as I waited for some sort of response from her father. I smiled back weakly just as the manager's door opened, revealing the flushed figure of the manager. Perspiration had formed like pustules on his forehead. It was a warm, but not a hot day.

"What do you want?" he said, and the way he said it, he made it sound like he really hated me. He didn't invite me in or anything, he just spoke to me right there in the doorway.

"I need to go home," I said. "I don't feel well," I told him, standing right there in the doorway. "I feel dizzy," I continued. This was a lie, as you know. I didn't feel dizzy, I felt dispirited. But I thought that feeling dizzy was a better reason to go home than feeling dispirited. And sometimes a lie is easier than the truth. I just wanted to go home and sleep; I couldn't bear the thought of even doing one more thing before I left.

The manager grunted moodily. He really was quite an unpleasant man, if I haven't made that clear enough already.

"OK," he said, as if he had about two million more important things to be doing. "Go home and rest. But you'd better not make a bloody habit of it."

He closed the door in my face, and by the way he closed the door in my face he made it clear that he really didn't like me too much. I couldn't really blame him. If I had been him I probably wouldn't have liked me too much either.

On my way out, the manager's daughter looked up from whatever she was doing. She smiled at me sympathetically.

"Hope you feel better," she said, sympathetically, and smiled.

Like I said, for some reason, she seemed to like me.

"Thanks," I said, and smiled back unconvincingly. I coughed a little bit to show that I was deserving of her sympathy.

It felt good to know that someone hoped I would feel better. I felt better all of a sudden. It raised my flagging spirits to know that someone seemed to like me and hoped that I would feel better.

"See you soon," she said.

"Bye," I said. "See you soon."

I walked home with a smile on my face.

My Brother Pays a Visit

'Mother must be worried about me,' I thought when I received news that my brother and his wife were to pay me a visit.

I knew that mother must have been worried about me because there was no other reason why my brother would pay me a visit. Mother must have asked him to. There was no other possible reason. It had been over a year since I had stolen hundreds of pounds from the girl I used to live with when I worked at the pie factory and left town quietly without telling anyone, and the only contact I'd had from him in that time was the terse letter informing me of the time and date that he intended to pay me a visit.

Mother must have asked him to send me a letter informing me of the time and date that he intended to pay me a visit, because he certainly wouldn't have done it of his own accord. I think it is fair to say that there were no feelings of affection lingering between my brother and me, if there had ever been any in the first place.

He arrived punctually at the exact time, almost to the minute, he had appointed to pay me a visit. He rang my buzzer but, finding it defunct, resorted to loudly and repeatedly banging on my front door with his fist.

I might have greeted him warmly, or at least politely, and invited him in had he not impatiently pushed his way past me as soon as I opened the door. He didn't like being kept waiting, even for a few seconds. He was known for being incredibly impatient. It was one of his things.

"Finally," he said indignantly, as if the indignity of having to wait, even for just a few seconds, for someone as inconsequential as me was more than he could bear. "I tried the buzzer, but it's broken. You should get it fixed," he continued, already marching up the communal staircase of the building in which I lived, without waiting for me to reply or lead the way.

His wife followed him inside, smiling at me sheepishly as if she was a student following the doctor on his rounds. I had met her once or twice before, but she looked somehow different from my memory of her. She possessed the kind of beauty that people who want to be seen as successful are attracted to. It was the kind of beauty that no one could argue with.

I followed the two of them into my flat feeling like I was being inspected, and suspecting that I would be found wanting in some significant respect. Once inside, my brother looked around the flat distastefully and curled his lip in disgust; his wife tried to pretend she hadn't noticed all the things that she had noticed.

I offered my guests a cup of tea. It was the least I could do and I always try to do at least the least that I can do. It's a bold sort of person who doesn't even do the least that they can do. And I am not a bold sort of person.

"Can I get you a cup of tea, or something?" I said. I offered a vague alternative to tea even though I had no alternative to tea, apart from water, which doesn't really count.

My brother spoke to his wife instead of answering me.

"Darling, would you mind?" he asked her blandly, like a man from the past.

My brother's wife was glad to have a distraction from the woeful figure that I presented, and the evident squalor of my existence. She rushed off to the kitchen to make tea. And now that my brother was standing there, in my flat, wearing his pristine suit and his shiny black leather shoes, looking rich and successful, it did seem quite a squalid existence. I had made no attempt to tidy up, even though I knew they were coming, and it did seem quite squalid, now that my brother was standing there in his pristine suit and his wife had rushed off to the kitchen to make tea. It hadn't done before but it did now.

I tried to imagine how my flat must have looked to my brother; my brother who had probably woken up in his own flat or house – house, probably – which was probably pristine like his suit, and was probably artfully furnished with fashionable brand new furniture.

I decided, without too much trouble, that, to my brother, it must have looked very squalid indeed.

I had no brand new furniture, only someone else's old furniture; furniture that was worn out and rickety: tables that wobbled precariously, chairs that felt like they could collapse at any moment, and a sofa that offered no support, that you sank unexpectedly into; a sofa that had probably been sat on by generations of wretched people living similarly squalid lives.

The carpet was discoloured to such an extent that it was hard to work out what colour it had once been. It was threadbare and there were several patches where there was almost no carpet left at all, only the threadbare skeleton of a carpet. There were several patches where it was hard to tell whether it was even a carpet at all.

The walls, too, had seen better days. It had not occurred to anyone to paint them for a number of years and they were covered in marks and stains.

Everything had seen better days; everything has always seen better days.

To add to the overall impression of neglect, detritus had congregated randomly on the floor: obsolete local newspapers were piled messily in one corner, discarded food wrappers were strewn around like the lifeless victims of a massacre; odd dust-covered socks were dotted around the room for no particular reason. An ashtray overflowed on a coffee table that was covered in a multitude of circles left behind by generations of cups and mugs.

It was a squalid and uncared for scene and I was actually surprised, as I tried to imagine how it must have looked through my brother's eyes that I hadn't noticed this before. It was quite apparent. It was really quite odd that I hadn't noticed it before.

My brother noticed all these things, and more too probably. He didn't sit down, but remained standing, as if he was not willing to commit himself to sitting down.

I had never known him to wear black leather driving gloves before, but as I remember it, he was wearing black leather driving gloves, the kind that can only be removed with deliberation. And, instead of sitting down, he was removing them with deliberation.

"Nice place you've got here," he said, after he had concluded his inspection of the room, but he didn't mean it.

I noticed that his hair was also shiny and black, like his shoes; he was sculpted in a painstaking fashion. He moved slowly and deliberately as if reluctant to disturb even a single hair on his head.

He looked rich. He smelt rich. He probably felt rich and tasted rich too. All he had ever wanted was money, so I guessed that he was happy, because he looked like he had lots of it.

'Good for you,' I thought, sarcastically.

From the kitchen came the sound of crockery and cutlery clattering together and the appalled groans of my brother's wife as she struggled with the festering mess that my kitchen had become. I didn't tidy up too often.

My brother looked towards the source of all these sounds and then back at me, his face displaying an instinctive disgust. I was everything he hated about other people, and he probably hated quite a lot about other people, which meant that he hated quite a lot about me.

It was time to get down to business. He fixed his gaze on me and rubbed his hands together. He was the kind of person who rubbed his hands together when it was time to get down to business, just to let you know that, as far as he was concerned, it was time to get down to business.

"Look," he said in a pristine, chiselled voice that matched his suit and his shoes. "Mother is very worried about you." If his voice had been a pair of shoes, it would have been a shiny black leather pair of shoes.

He paused dramatically and started pacing to and fro at a funereal pace. I was sitting, sunken, on the depressed sofa and he looked down at me whenever he could bear to.

"It's just not good enough. As if the poor woman hasn't got enough to worry about."

From the kitchen could be heard the sound of a kettle being filled. "She cares about you; you're her son, for God's sake! Of course she cares about you." The clear implication was that there was no other possible reason why anyone would care about me.

"You don't call. You don't write. You don't visit," he said, listing the charges against me, counting them on his fingers, as if everything was my fault.

"She thinks you're depressed. She thinks you're going to, you know, top yourself or something. She talks about nothing else. If you could hear her, you'd call at least. And father's ill, really ill this time. It looks like this is it for him. He's really ill. It's all too much for her to take. It's all too much."

He gave me an accusatory look as if father's illness was the result of some treachery on my part.

"She really has got enough to worry about."

He coughed a little, probably unnecessary, cough.

"She's a shadow of herself, you know, these days."

The kettle could be heard beginning its crescendo.

"She hardly leaves the house anymore."

To tell the truth I did almost feel a little sorry for mother. She had tried her best and had probably never meant anyone any actual harm. She was a good person; or at least she wasn't a bad person.

"She's put on a lot of weight."

The kettle began to spit and roar in the agitated and frenetic manner in which the kettles of the time spat and roared.

"Father leaving hit her pretty hard, you know that. And now his illness. And you're not helping. You're not helping at all. It's just selfish. You need to start thinking about someone other than yourself for a change." He paused, as if his displeasure was so great that he had to pause, to collect himself. "It's all down to me, isn't it? I visit at least once a week. Sometimes twice. I make sure she's OK. It's always me that has to pick up the pieces."

He stared at me as if he expected thanks, as if he wanted me to acknowledge what a great son he was. He certainly was dutiful, I'll give him that. He always did what was expected of him. He may have been a massive bastard, but he was, at least, a dutiful massive bastard. And punctual. Don't forget punctual. He had many admirable qualities.

He put his hand to his head and his golden wristwatch gleamed, even though the light in my flat was gloomy at the best of times. It was one of those flats that are gloomy even at the best of times. It had small windows that tended to face walls and other windows, rather than sources of light. Any light it did receive was reflected.

The kettle became increasingly agitated.

"Can't we put the bloody lights on?" my brother said, irritably. I made no effort to move so he looked around for the light switch. He found it and turned the light on. The cold unforgiving electrical light made my flat look even grimmer. He resumed his position in front of me.

"She talks about you all the bloody time. You've got no idea, you know, what I have to listen to." He looked at me as if it was all my fault. "It's not much fun, let me tell you. 'Stealing money from his girlfriend.'" His voice shifted up in pitch, imitating the querulous tone that always infected our mother's voice when she was upset about something. And it was a pretty good impression too. It sounded like he had been practising. "'Living on his own in a strange town. And running away without telling anyone. Oh, I'm so worried about him.' I tell you, I've heard it all about a thousand bloody times! Can't you just bloody call her, at least? Tell her you're doing great; tell her you've got a girlfriend; tell her you've got a good job; tell her anything so she doesn't have to bloody worry about you anymore. It's not right to do this to her; it's just not bloody right." He shook his head. He was the kind of person who said 'bloody' a lot when he wanted you to know he was angry about something. He wouldn't just sound angry like most people would, he would say 'bloody' a lot instead.

The kettle was roaring and shaking as if it was about to take off. I remember that kettle; it really did make a hell of a racket. And it took its time boiling water too. It refused to be rushed. It was stubborn as hell.

My brother stood expectantly in front of me.

"Well?" he said, his eyes widening. "Come on! Haven't you got anything to bloody well say for yourself?"

From the kitchen came the sound of very hot water being poured into mugs, not that it really matters. The sound of very hot water being poured into mugs has absolutely nothing to do with anything whatsoever.

"I'll call her later," I said, when the sound of very hot water being poured into mugs had stopped. I had to say something. It was clear that he expected me to say something.

He laughed scornfully, which was the only way he ever seemed to laugh when he was around me. His mocking scornful laugh was the only laugh of his I knew. I'm sure he had other laughs, but I never heard them. He rubbed his forehead with his hand; his golden wristwatch gleamed in the unforgiving light, and it was an unforgiving gleam.

The sound of mugs of tea being stirred.

The sound of three mugs being picked up with two hands.

The two mugs being held by the same hand clinked together.

"Clink," said one of the mugs.

"Clink, clink," said the other mug. It was almost like the mugs were having a conversation.

Not that it matters.

"Clink, clink, clink, clink, clink."

My brother's wife appeared in the doorway advancing cautiously, her eyes fixed on the brimming mugs of tea, taking extraordinary care not to spill a drop. I didn't care whether she spilt a drop or not, and I might have told her not to worry about spilling a drop, but I didn't. I could see the trouble she was having, and thought about telling her not to worry about spilling a drop, but didn't.

She placed one of the mugs on a small table next to my brother. Having looked around for a coaster without success, she settled on carefully placing the mug on an obsolete local newspaper.

"Thank you, darling," said my brother.

It would really piss me off if someone called me 'darling' like that, but she didn't seem to mind.

She handed me my cup of tea and I placed it on the floor. She went and stood next to my brother, holding her mug gingerly in front of her. Like her husband she opted not to sit down. There were chairs. They could both have sat down if they had wanted to, but they obviously didn't want to.

My brother took a sip of his still too hot to drink tea. It seemed to scold him and he flinched a little. The cup of tea was on my side. We were a team, the cup of tea and I. Good old cup of tea.

"What the bloody hell are you going to do with your life?" he said, looking at me contemptuously, as if he couldn't imagine what I was possibly going to do with my life.

I didn't reply, because I couldn't think of a single thing to say.

There was a moment of awkward silence, which he probably didn't find awkward at all.

'I'm going to try not to draw attention to myself,' I thought listlessly.

Phoning Mother

After my brother and his wife left, which they did promptly after finishing their cups of tea, I put on some reasonably clean socks, slipped on a pair of shitty tennis shoes, rustled some change together and went down to the public pay phone on the corner of the street.

I certainly didn't want my brother paying me another visit and would have done a lot more than phone mother to avoid it, even if it did make my brother look like the good guy. 'But,' I reasoned, 'it really isn't worth worrying about what anyone who thinks my brother is the good guy thinks about anything.'

Anyone who thinks my brother is the good guy clearly lacks judgement.

The phone box smelt of stale urine and the passing of time, not that it really matters.

I inserted the change I had rustled together into the slot and dialled my mother's number. It was the only phone number I knew by heart. It is the only phone number I have ever known by heart.

She answered immediately. "Hello," she said tentatively, as if answering the telephone for the very first time.

"Hello mother, it's me," I said, trying to sound like a proper human being.

"Who?" she said, as if she had never spoken to me before, and had no idea who I was.

I hadn't expected to have to explain who I was; I thought she would recognise my voice.

"It's me, your son," I said, raising my voice slightly in case it was a bad line. The lines in public pay phones were often bad lines.

"Oh, hello love. How are you?" she said, sounding old and vulnerable, which made me feel pretty rotten. She sounded quite excited in her own old and vulnerable way.

She told me how glad she was to hear from me, which was very glad, and told me how worried she'd been about me, which was very worried.

I lied my arse off that day on the bad line in the phone box that smelt of stale urine and the passing of time.

"Yeah, it was great to see him," I lied.

"It's good money and there's loads of opportunities for promotion," I said, deceitfully.

"I'll definitely come and visit soon," I continued shamelessly, making a promise that I had no intention of keeping.

"Well, there's a girl I'm seeing, but it's nothing too serious at the moment. We're just having fun."

Lying to your mother about your sex life is the lowest form of bullshit in the world. I'm sure not too many people would argue with that.

"OK, I've got to go. I'm meeting some friends in town," I said. The lies kept coming. My deception knew no bounds; it had no shame.

"OK, then. Bye love. Keep in touch now," said mother, more than happy to believe all my rotten lies.

"I will," I lied. I had no intention of keeping in touch. "Bye mother."

Christmas Party

It was the Christmas party. I know it was the Christmas party because I can remember the hats. We were all wearing Christmas hats.

The manager's daughter had insisted that I attend. For some reason that I couldn't quite fathom, she seemed to be nurturing some sort of affection for me.

If she hadn't insisted that I attend the Christmas party, I never would have gone. But she did insist and so, one night, in the week or weeks preceding a Christmas, I found myself sitting around a table with the other people who worked at the same place as me, wearing a Christmas hat.

I decided to drink until the situation became almost bearable, as I could think of no other way to make the situation almost bearable.

I was sat next to the manager's daughter and opposite her father, the manager. There were other people around the table, but they made no difference to me at all and I can't remember a single thing about any of them. It seems likely that at least one or two of them had brown hair, or wore glasses, or had a beard, or something like that. But I can't be sure.

I was already quite drunk when the manager's daughter, who was sitting next to me, started stroking my thigh. Her touches were light and sporadic at first, like someone waiting for a bus, but as time passed and her glass emptied they lingered and became heavier, like someone waiting for a train.

I was getting pretty excited to tell the truth. It had been a long time since anyone had done anything like stroking my thigh.

The meal started awkwardly. Despite the manager's injunction that no one talked about work, the people round the table had little in common apart from the fact that they all worked together, so most people talked about work.

The only exception was the manager's daughter who had an assortment of things to say on a variety of other subjects. She was talking to me, but you couldn't have really called it a conversation because I wasn't saying much. In fact, I was hardly even nodding to show that I was listening, or making any other gesture to show that I was listening, because I wasn't really listening. I was far too busy being excited by the fact that she was stroking my thigh as she spoke to me. It had been years since anyone had stroked my thigh, or done anything like stroking my thigh.

By the time the main course was cleared away, she was sitting so close to me that her mouth almost touched my ear as she spoke. Her hot breath made me shiver; it almost tickled, and I almost laughed once or twice.

I felt an overwhelming desire that threatened to overwhelm me. I wondered if it was my lucky day. I wondered if I was in love.

Her hand moved slowly up my thigh until it was resting on my private parts.

I placed my hand on her black-stockinged thigh and rubbed it clumsily.

"Oh!" she exclaimed, as if shocked by my audacity, but I don't think she really was. I think it would have taken something pretty outrageous to really shock her.

Her exclamation was loud enough to attract the attention of her father who, in case you have forgotten, was also the manager.

He glowered suspiciously at us both. He was good at glowering suspiciously. It was like glowering suspiciously had been made just for him.

"You all right?" he asked his daughter suspiciously, as if he suspected her of enjoying herself a little too much, which was not something the manager was disposed to tolerate.

"Oh yes, I'm fine, don't you worry about me," the manager's daughter replied dismissively, barely even turning to face her father. She laughed into my ear, her hot breath rippling through my body. It tickled and I couldn't help laughing.

The manager continued to scowl at me for quite a few more seconds, before resuming the conversation he was having with the two men sitting next to him. I have no idea what they were talking about, but I'm sure you can imagine a suitable topic for their conversation. I don't know: football or work, or something like that.

Whatever it was about, the manager clearly wasn't able to give the conversation his full attention. He kept looking over at us. As far as he was concerned, we were enjoying each other's company a little too much, and he didn't like it. It was making it hard for him to concentrate. He kept looking over at us and scowling. The manager was pretty good at scowling; it was almost as if scowling had been invented just for him.

He couldn't take it any longer; he wanted it to stop. He abruptly tapped his wine glass with a knife; it made a dinging sound, like this: 'DIIIINNNNGGGGGGGG!'

And then he started speaking.

"OK," he said. "First of all, I'd like to thank you all for coming." Everyone else round the table had stopped talking and leaned forward to hear what the manager had to say, as if they expected the manager to have something interesting or funny to say. The manager's daughter's hand still rested on my private parts and stroked them gently, while she stared provocatively at her father.

The manager's daughter's father continued speaking.

"And I'd like to thank everyone for their hard work this year. And I think it's been a damn good year for us. And next year promises to be even better." The manager, who had quickly reached the extent of his speechmaking powers and had nothing else to say, paused. "Um," he said, after a pause. "So, cheers, everybody," he continued. "Happy Christmas."

The manager raised his glass and everyone else raised their glasses also, apart from his daughter and I, who had other things to do.

"Happy Christmas," said everyone in unison, but at slightly different times.

Then the manager thought of something else to say. He looked at me and continued speaking.

"And I'd like to, um, take this opportunity to invite our newest member of staff to say a few words," he said, looking at me and gesturing towards me, to make it clear he was talking about me. "Just tell us how you've found the company. A Christmas tradition. We've all done it." A few faces round the table exchanged confused looks, but went along with it and didn't say anything. The manager was the kind of guy you just went along with if you possibly could.

I suddenly felt a little sick. I couldn't think of a single thing to say.

The table was quiet. The manager looked at me complacently, as if he had achieved everything he set out to achieve, which he probably had. The others – the people he managed, everyone else - looked at me expectantly, as if they expected me to say something interesting or funny, which there was very little chance of.

The manager's daughter scowled at her father. She was good at it too; she had inherited her father's talents.

"Come on," said the manager. "Just a few words."

I had to say something. I would have said something interesting or funny if I could have done, but I really couldn't think of a single interesting or funny thing to say.

"I'm not sure. What do you want me to say? I'm not sure what you want me to say," I said, because I had to say something, and I honestly didn't know what else to say.

The manager laughed hysterically, as if I had just told the funniest joke he had ever heard. But he was laughing at me, not with me, as people say. Unintentionally, I had amused him. His whole body shook; the table shook; the crockery shook; the whole restaurant probably shook; maybe birds hundreds of miles away were blown ever so slightly off course for a moment or two.

The manager slapped the man next to him on the back urging him to join in, which he duly did, though, inevitably, he lacked some of the manager's enthusiasm.

I felt my face turning bright red. I felt blood rush to my cheeks, and my ears felt hot. If the manager's daughter's hands had been cold she might have been able to warm them by holding them near my ears.

The laughter eventually died down; it couldn't go on forever. That's the thing with laughter: it can't go on forever.

There was a moment of awkward silence while we all waited for the manager to compose himself enough to say something else, but before he could do so his daughter urged him to leave me alone.

The manager's daughter: my knight in shining armour.

"Leave him alone," she said. "You're just a bloody bully." She sounded genuinely upset and angry. I thought she might start crying. "You just can't stand anyone else having fun, can you?" she said. "Can you?" she repeated but louder, angrier.

"Oh please," her father said. He snorted. "Am I a bully?" he asked the man to his left.

"Oh no," said the man to his left, shaking his head as if it was the most ridiculous thing he had ever heard anyone say.

"Am I a bully?" the manager asked the man to his right.

"No, absolutely not," said the man to his right decisively, as if it was the only thing in his entire life that he was a hundred per cent certain of.

"Well then," said the manager as if he had proved beyond all reasonable doubt, and to everyone's satisfaction, that he was definitely not a bully.

His daughter sighed angrily. She was holding back tears of frustration and anger. She looked away, into the air, anywhere but at the manager. Her hands were no longer anywhere near my private parts.

The manager seemed satisfied by this arrangement. He turned his attention back to me.

"So, tell me, why'd you decide to work in a warehouse? It can't be much fun down there," he said, goading me, and looking at me with contempt. All eyes turned in my direction.

I had to say something.

"Money, I guess," I said, because I had to say something and because there was no other plausible answer.

The manager's expression of contempt dissolved into one of hearty amusement.

"And you don't get much of that!" he said. "I should know!" He thought this was funny. He thought someone not earning a lot of money was funny. That's the kind of person he was. He laughed like an idiot, as if this was the funniest thing anyone had ever said, which it definitely wasn't, not by a long way. Most of the other people round the table laughed too. They had to really; they didn't really have a choice. It would have been almost confrontational to allow the manager to laugh like that on his own. They were probably just being polite.

The manager's daughter huffed noisily. I felt unbearably silly. It was hugely embarrassing. Even though I was drunk I felt hugely embarrassed.

The laughter died down.

It seemed that there was nothing else to say because nothing else was said. There was a brief uncomfortable pause during which the manager looked at me with grim satisfaction. It was a look that seemed to imply that there was plenty more where that came from if I dared enjoy his daughter's company too much again.

The people round the table resumed their conversations; the manager's daughter continued looking away into the air. She no longer seemed to be holding back tears of frustration and anger. She had cooled and hardened.

I bowed my head and closed my eyes. My eyes snapped shut; my head was spinning. I had drunk too much. I heard snatches of conversation, though I couldn't tell who was talking or where the voices were coming from; disembodied voices surrounded me.

"… keep forgetting about her …" said one voice.

"… no, I don't, the thing is …" said another voice.

"… I can't bear it, I really can't …"

I wanted to go home. I wanted to leave but I wasn't sure how to go about leaving, because my eyes were closed and my head was spinning, and disembodied voices surrounded me.

Suddenly it was all over. Somehow, I was vaguely aware of people standing around me. My eyes opened slightly revealing a blurry unstable version of reality. All that I could decipher was that the meal was over and people were standing up to leave.

I attempted to stand up so that I wasn't the only one left sitting at the table. Trying not to draw attention to myself had become a deeply ingrained habit, which not even drink could dull. It had become instinctive.

The attempt, however, was unsuccessful. I fell with a thud to the floor. As I fell I grabbed onto the table and it began to topple. A fork fell on my head, but luckily the manager's daughter managed to steady the table before its entire contents clattered to the floor.

She helped me to my feet, which was good of her. She didn't have to do that.

I'm sure that people were laughing at me, but I can't be sure.

I felt sick. I stood unsteadily, swaying from side to side, before vomiting dirty reddish-blackish vomit all over the table. If people had been laughing at me before, their laughter would have turned to groans of disgust.

I wiped my mouth, looked around wildly, and staggered from the restaurant without conscious thought, like a captive animal unexpectedly freed. Instinct alone guided my steps.

The manager, the manager's daughter, and the others watched me leave with shocked, outraged or disgusted expressions. How shocked, how outraged, or how disgusted I will let you judge for yourself.

I staggered from the restaurant and disappeared into the darkness of a long winter's night. Goodbye Christmas party; hello darkness of a long winter's night.

Dead Duck

I wasn't going to tell you about this, but I guess I should. I think it might be important. You never know what might be important, but I think this might be.

I was a mere child at the time. I was too young to be held accountable. I was too young to be blamed for anything I did. I didn't know any better and there was no way I could have been expected to know any better. No way at all.

My family had gone on holiday to this holiday village that we used to go to. My parents had taken me along because I was, whether they liked it or not, a member of the family, and a mere child who certainly couldn't be left at home to fend for myself.

In order to keep me occupied and not too much of a bother, I had been allowed to bring a friend, and so I had brought a friend.

One of the few things I knew about my friend was that his parents had once been quite rich but had lost a lot of money in some disastrous business venture that went horribly wrong. My friend would sometimes obscurely refer to this disaster but never openly discussed it. He never went into details. Not that I asked him to. I didn't.

When they had been quite rich my friend's parents had sent him to an expensive private school, but after they lost a lot of money in the disastrous business venture that went horribly wrong, they could no longer afford the fees and he had to leave. And so one day he arrived at my school wearing a green hunting jacket with three cigars in the pocket that he had stolen from his father. The cigars, I mean. I think the jacket was his. In any case, if it wasn't, his father definitely didn't mind him borrowing it because he wore it all the time. He never took it off, even when a teacher or his mother asked him to. He just refused.

All of the other kids at school thought he was a jerk and stayed out of his way, which was fine with him because he thought they were all jerks too.

Most people think most people are jerks, and they're probably right if you want to know the truth.

I thought he was a jerk too, but I thought most people were jerks and I liked the kind of jerk he was. He was my kind of jerk.

We smoked cigars, which I don't think either of us particularly enjoyed, in the woods at the back of the school playground. We got caught a couple of times but neither of us cared too much. Mother was a little disappointed when she got the phone call from the school informing her that her son had been caught smoking a cigar in the woods at the back of the school playground, and she told me so repeatedly, but it wasn't too bad. It was worth it to smoke cigars that I didn't particularly enjoy with someone who was my kind of jerk.

He thought my family was brilliant. I think this was probably because we were all such a bunch of bastards. Apart from mother, I guess. I don't think she ever meant too much harm to anyone. But the rest of us were definitely a bunch of bastards, and I think that is why he thought we were brilliant. We amused him.

His family were always terribly polite to each other and had terribly sophisticated conversations about books, and what they'd done that day, and what they thought about this or that, whereas we were forever cursing and fighting so that anyone would have thought we hated each other's guts, which I think it's fair to say we probably did. Anyway, he thought it was brilliant.

Maybe it was.

He was the kind of person who was good with people. I've always been a little in awe of people like that, probably because I am not that kind of person at all. He just instinctively knew how to get people to like him. It was quite a skill.

He was always flawlessly polite to my mother and she thought him quite the cultivated little charmer when he quoted some saying or other, or complimented her on her choice of outfit, or the way she did her hair, or a subtle innovation in the way she applied her make-up that no one else had noticed. He did notice things. He was good like that.

He called her 'mum', which made me feel sick, but which mother thought was adorable. No one else called her 'mum'. My brother and I called her 'mother', which she didn't seem to think was too adorable.

When he was talking to father, he laughed indulgently at all his witticisms as if they were the funniest witticisms he had ever heard, which I very much doubt they were. He talked to my father about hunting: the thrill of the chase, and the excitement of a kill, the woods, the smell of blood in the morning air. My friend's parents used to go hunting, and had taken him along once or twice. Father listened in awed, subservient silence, as someone who knows nothing about a subject listens to another who they regard as something of an expert, and treated him with courtesy and respect, even letting him smoke his cigars on the patio, while looking on approvingly.

"He's a good lad, that one," he would say as he looked on approvingly. The clear implication was that I wasn't.

He also got on very well with my brother. In fact, they got on better with each other than either of them did with me and, because they got on so well, I was quite often left alone, or with my parents, which was worse.

I didn't have a great time on that holiday, it must be said. It wasn't the greatest time I ever had.

On our third or fourth night at the holiday village, my brother met a girl at the disco.

They had a disco at the holiday village. It was an embarrassment really. If I had been that disco I'd have been embarrassed to call myself a disco. It was sandwiched between a bowling alley and a restaurant. It wasn't a great disco.

When he returned from the disco on our third or fourth night at the holiday village, my brother told me and my friend that he had touched a girl's breasts. He told us this with great pride as if it was a real achievement, as if people didn't touch girls' breasts every goddamn day, as if at any moment of the goddamn day there weren't about twenty million people touching a girl's breasts.

The following day he brought her to the chalet we were staying in to show her off. She was pretty, I had to admit, even though I didn't want to, and I felt pretty rotten that it was my brother touching her breasts and not me.

They said they were going on a bike ride, and mother made them some sandwiches, which she wrapped in foil and placed urgently in my brother's rucksack, as if placing the sandwiches in my brother's rucksack was a matter of the utmost urgency.

As they left my brother winked at my friend and I, and I knew that within five minutes he'd be fingering her in a nearby bush, rudely wagging his tongue in her mouth and groping her breasts. I didn't know much but I knew enough to know that. He had absolutely no sense of romance. I was more than a little jealous.

My parents left a few minutes later to 'enjoy the facilities', as father said, which meant that I had the friend that I had brought on the family holiday to myself, which was definitely better than being alone all day, or being stuck with my parents. There was, after all, a reason why I had brought him on the family holiday. I sort of enjoyed his company. He was my kind of jerk, like I said.

After my parents left we sat on the green plastic furniture that adorned the chalet's small square patio area and smoked cigars. The small square patio area led down to a picturesque little lake fringed by cycle tracks and little shrubs, which was populated by a multitude of ducks that had forgotten the taste of fear. They had forgotten the taste of fear because they were holiday ducks and had nothing to fear.

The ducks wandered casually amongst the chalets, as if human beings could not possibly pose any danger to them, which I suppose, generally speaking, they didn't. The ducks wandered freely; the human beings posed no danger. That was the way it worked; that was the way it had always worked at the holiday village.

The friend that I had brought on the family holiday took an instant dislike to these ducks on account of their fearlessness. He wanted them to fear him. Their indifference simply wouldn't do, so when one of the ducks wandered heedlessly onto our patio area he slapped it across the face to teach it a lesson. It quacked away surprised, as if being slapped across the face was something it had never even thought about.

He then began throwing fir cones and flicking matches at the ducks; he laughed happily as they scurried away wondering what the hell was going on. Things like this didn't normally happen to the ducks at the holiday village. They were unaccustomed to such unwarranted acts of aggression. They were holiday ducks, after all, and had got used to having nothing to fear.

The ducks quacked nervously.

"Quack!" the ducks said nervously.

I think at first I felt an instinctive sympathy for the helpless and slightly panicked ducks, who were unaccustomed to such unwarranted acts of aggression and had got used to having nothing to fear. But my friend had an infectious personality and he made me feel that, really, throwing things at ducks was what life was all about.

"Come on, have a go," he said, as if I was obstinately refusing to do something that he knew I would enjoy. He threw a fir cone at me. And another. He flicked a match at me. "Come on," he insisted.

I was powerless to resist such cajoling.

I gripped one of the fir cones in my hand and threw it wildly at a duck that wasn't too close, knowing that I would most probably miss, which I did.

"Here," said the friend that I had brought on the family holiday, handing me another fir cone. "Have another go. Try and hit that one." He pointed at a duck that was wandering vaguely towards us, pausing every so often to take a closer look at the ground.

I took aim and threw the fir cone. It bounced off the head of the stunned duck, which quacked frantically away, looking in all directions at once.

"Quack!" said the stunned duck frantically. "Quack!" it said again, looking in all directions at once. It might have looked bewildered, but it's hard to read the facial expressions of ducks. They don't give too much away.

After the cigars had been reduced to ashes, we took our bikes out for a bike ride. Everyone was always cycling everywhere at the holiday village. We rode out into the woods, stopping every so often to chuck stones, fir cones, sticks, or whatever was to hand, at squirrels or rabbits or whatever small animals happened to be unfortunate enough to cross our path.

Eventually, we stopped by a picturesque little waterfall that emptied itself into a picturesque little lake. We sat on a rock, throwing stones into the picturesque little lake, watching the splashes with satisfaction as they hit the water below.

"Your brother's pretty cool, I reckon," said my friend, having decided to tell me that he thought my brother was pretty cool.

"He's a total prick when you get to know him," I said.

"You think everyone's a prick."

"So do you."

"Well I reckon he's pretty cool. You're lucky to have a brother like that."

We tacitly agreed to disagree. It was one of those situations where neither person was likely to agree with the other. Our minds were made up.

It went pretty quiet after that.

My friend began collecting stones and piling them up into a little pile. When he had collected an appreciable amount, he took a handful and put them in my jacket pocket. It was summer and not cold, but I always wore a jacket so I could carry things in its pockets and because I felt sorry for the jacket.

It was a yellow jacket and, although I didn't realise when I bought it, it was a woman's jacket. I didn't realise it was a woman's jacket until someone I knew laughed at me for wearing a yellow woman's jacket. Apparently wearing a yellow woman's jacket was funny, but I didn't particularly care too much. In fact the mocking laughter of someone I knew only made me become even more attached to the jacket. The thought of discarding it because it was yellow, and a women's jacket, made me want to cry. I had a real emotional connection to that jacket, for some reason. It even got to the point where I wanted to cry and felt sorry for the jacket if I saw it on the back of a chair or in a crumpled mess on the floor. If that happened I usually just put the jacket on, which was easier than wanting to cry and feeling sorry for the jacket.

I thought it made me look like a pop star.

And I actually thought that the more I wore it the less yellow and the less womanly it would become. But I wore it quite a lot and it didn't become any less yellow, or any less womanly.

"Come on then, let's go and throw stones at things," said my friend resignedly as if there was nothing else in the world that we could possibly do, as if throwing stones at things was our only option.

He led the way and stood at the top of the picturesque little waterfall that emptied itself into the picturesque little lake below. It was all very unreal; it was nothing at all like reality.

The friend that I had brought on the family holiday scanned the vicinity looking for targets. The natural world, for him, was full of targets. There was a trio of ducks maundering at the foot of the picturesque little waterfall and there were occasional rabbits darting here and there, but never hanging around for too long. The ducks had forgotten the taste of fear, but the rabbits clearly had longer memories and were on their guard at all times.

It was a fine cloudless summer's day, still and sweet.

My friend saw a rabbit cautiously nibbling on something as it looked around warily, taking no unnecessary risks. He took aim. He threw a stone at the rabbit, but missed. The rabbit had disappeared before the stone even landed. It was on its guard and was taking no unnecessary risks. The rabbit was wary and knew how to look after itself. It was not an easy target.

"Little bastard," said my friend, as if it was the rabbit's fault that he had missed.

He then turned his attention to the trio of ducks maundering at the foot of the picturesque little waterfall. They moved slowly and had forgotten the taste of fear, which made them an easy target. He closed one eye and leant back. He grunted as he launched his missile with some ferocity towards the ducks. But his stone splashed harmlessly into the little lake nowhere near its target. The ducks didn't even seem to notice, and continued to show no signs of wariness. I wanted to warn them; I wanted to shout 'Look out!' or something like that, but it probably wouldn't have done much good. They probably would have just ignored me.

Meanwhile, I had started listlessly chucking the stones that my friend had put into the pocket of my yellow woman's jacket, which I felt sorry for, towards a nearby tree. The friend that I had brought on the family holiday flung a withering look at me.

"Stop wasting stones," he said, as if there was a shortage of stones or something. "You can't hurt a tree."

He again took aim at the trio of ducks who continued to maunder at the foot of the waterfall. He adjusted his aim slightly after his previous failed attempt and this time hit one of the ducks on its backside. The duck seemed rather taken aback, as if it had never imagined that being hit on the backside by a stone was a thing that could possibly happen. It quacked and glided away quickly, displaying a hitherto unseen agility, settling a few metres away from the other two ducks.

"Yesssss!" hissed my friend. He punched the air as if hitting the duck was a real accomplishment.

The other two ducks looked over at the now lone duck but didn't seem too concerned. They were busy maundering and imminent danger wasn't something they knew too much about, or had even imagined.

"Right, your turn," said my friend, turning to me as if he had proved himself beyond all doubt and now it was my turn to prove myself beyond all doubt.

I was helpless in the face of such cajoling.

I picked a small smooth stone out of my jacket pocket.

I had no intention of the small smooth stone making contact with any of the ducks below. No intention at all.

I leant back and spun my arm in a cartoonish fashion. I closed my eyes and released the small smooth stone without any thought of taking aim. It was a wild reckless moment: a moment without intent.

The stone flew viciously through the air.

I opened my eyes as it struck one of ducks right in the middle of its head.

I'm going to call him – I guessed it was a him, for some reason – Peter. That wasn't his real name but, for some reason, that is what I am going to call him.

Peter started screaming. Not quacking. Screaming.

"Aaaggghhhh!" said Peter. "Aaaggghhhh!"

Peter was screaming and thrashing about wildly and blindly in all directions at once, as if his whole world had shattered; as if everything he had ever known was broken and no longer made any sense.

"Oh, wow!" said my friend who was dividing his attention between the wildly, blindly thrashing duck and me, his mouth agape. "No way!" he said happily, hardly able to contain himself. He was clearly very pleased with the way things were going.

He slapped me on the back, which almost sent me flying, and started scrambling down the side of the waterfall towards where Peter had now ceased his violent thrashing and just floated, tragically, face down in the water. I followed in his wake.

When we reached the bottom of the slope Peter was bobbing lifelessly against the bank of the lake. My friend crouched down, planting his feet firmly, and fished him out of the water. He placed Peter on the grass.

We stood there with our hands on our knees breathing heavily, examining with fascination the startled duck with the faintest of pulses, clinging onto life: Peter.

"You've got to put it out of its misery. You're going to have to break its neck," said my friend authoritatively, in the style of somebody who knows what they're talking about, and I had no reason to doubt that he knew what he was talking about.

"I can't do that," I said, knowing that I wouldn't be able to break Peter's neck, even if that was what I had to do. "Can't you do it? Haven't you done this kind of thing before?" I asked, beginning to feel cold and shaky at the thought of having to break Peter's neck.

My friend acted as if offended by my assumption that he had done something like break a dying duck's neck before.

"I might shoot stuff," he said, as if other living creatures were just stuff. "But I don't go round strangling ducks. I'm not some sort of psychopath."

"Can't we just bury it?" I asked meekly, imagining that if I wasn't able to break Peter's neck, I might just about be able to bury a duck that wasn't quite dead.

"It's still bloody well alive," he said, as if I was an idiot, which I probably was, which I definitely was when it came to strangling ducks, or burying things that weren't quite dead.

"It's still alive," he said again, but a little more pensively this time.

'*He's* still alive,' I thought. '*Peter's* still alive.'

The friend that I had brought on the family holiday stepped on Peter's neck with the heel of his shoe. He pressed down hard putting all of his weight into it. Then he bent down and placed his index and middle finger on Peter's stepped-on neck.

"It's dead," he said. "It's stopped breathing."

'*Peter's* dead,' I thought. '*Peter's* stopped breathing.'

Thankfully, my friend had taken control of the situation. He picked Peter up carefully and scampered up a gently rising slope into a thicket. If he hadn't taken control of the situation, I have absolutely no idea what I would have done.

He seemed to be quite enjoying himself. He seemed to enjoy having life and death in his hands. He placed Peter delicately on the ground, showing more respect to his lifeless body than I had expected him to.

We dug a shallow grave with our hands. The earth was soft and moist, and lodged itself in our fingernails as if hoping at some opportune moment to give us away, to reveal with incontestable evidence the identity of Peter's killer and his accomplice.

The hole was probably less than a foot deep. It seemed like there was no time to lose, and so we didn't dig any deeper. We placed Peter in the little hole and I said a little prayer in my head. It was all as respectful as it could possibly have been.

We were awed in the presence of death.

As we covered him up and he vanished gradually from sight forever, I swear I saw him breath. I'm sure we buried that duck alive.

I'm sure we buried *Peter* alive.

We didn't hang around after that. Instead we ran back to where we had left our bikes and sped away.

I think before that moment life had seemed to me like some sort of fantasy, but if it had, it was a fantasy no longer.

As we sped away I felt light and heavy at the same time. My body seemed airy as if it might float away at any moment. I barely noticed its motions. The rapid pedalling caused me no fatigue at all. But my mind felt like a leaden weight and I couldn't think about anything without great effort, as if my consciousness was a great intricate machine with innumerable cogs and pistons, levers and pulleys that I had no idea how to operate.

As we rode speedily through the woods, trees rushing by, away from our guilty secret, I heard voices whirling around my head. I heard the voice of my father admonishing me, the voice of my mother scolding me, the voice of my brother mocking me, and other voices that I didn't recognise saying things I couldn't quite make out.

The voices whirled around my head. I pretty much thought I was going insane. I pretty much thought that was it for me.

We rode back to the chalet without stopping or speaking. When we got there my parents had returned and were watching a game show in the living room, my father shouting out all the wrong answers and making vulgar comments about the contestants. But I wasn't really paying attention. All I could think about was Peter and I imagined the details of his murder were written all over my face for anyone to see.

I went to the bathroom and locked the door. I examined myself in the mirror. I looked different; I looked like me, but a pale anguished me. I was haunted; Peter haunted me. His image was fixed before my eyes, his dying, frantic, recriminatory look.

'You killed me,' it seemed to say. 'Never will I maunder again, you bastard.'

That evening I snuck out of the chalet and cycled to the holiday village's church. It didn't amount to much, but the holiday village had its own church.

In the near darkness of a summer evening, the church was populated only by shadows. I sat on a pew near the back next to a family of shadows who were already sitting there.

I knelt down and begged God for forgiveness and said a prayer for Peter, because I still believed in stuff like that then and thought it might help. It was too late to help Peter but I thought it might help me. Somehow.

I hadn't meant to kill Peter and I felt sure that God would understand. I thought I had a pretty tight relationship with God in those days.

After all, I hadn't meant to kill Peter. There was no way it was murder; at worst it was duck slaughter. It was a crazy accident, a foolish youthful indiscretion.

'Everyone makes mistakes,' I thought, 'especially when they're young.' I was not to blame; there was no way I could be blamed. I was too young to be blamed for anything.

'Yes,' I thought hopefully. 'God will definitely understand.' After all, we were pretty tight back then.

Part Two

The Market Research Company

The market research company crouched amongst the shadows of other taller buildings, as if it was trying to keep out of sight. It was accessed via a rank alleyway that had fallen out with the sun.

It was as if the market research company was playing hide-and-seek with the world and had found a really good hiding place.

One of the buildings was furnished with rows of telephones and banks of computer screens; row upon row, bank upon bank.

'Here's your telephone and there's your computer screen,' I imagined someone would say when you started working at the market research company.

Somehow I had found out that you could get a job there without too much trouble.

And so one morning I found myself in a white-walled, low-ceiled room about to be trained as a 'telephone interviewer'.

It was one of those rooms that on first glance looks reasonably well maintained, but that a closer inspection reveals to be in a state of systematic neglect; it looked like it had been left out in the rain.

The man who the market research company had employed to train 'telephone interviewers' was standing in front of me. It was clear from his manner that he was about to start doing something, and that the thing he was about to start doing was a thing he had done many times before.

The man was pale-faced; it didn't look like his face had seen the sun too often. He had long fair hair and a wispy goatee beard too if you're interested, which seems unlikely.

I guess he was in his middle-twenties, or middle-thirties, but it was hard to tell. He was the kind of person who was probably in his middle-twenties, but who you wouldn't be too surprised to learn was actually in his middle-thirties.

And he was the kind of person who wore shorts even when it was cold outside. He was the kind of person who wore shorts whatever the weather, and yet still seemed to be permanently covered by a film of perspiration.

There were also other people in the room who I could only imagine were there for the same reason as me. We were all looking up at the pale-faced man who had now started explaining how to be a 'telephone interviewer' for the market research company.

At several moments during that morning I fantasised about sneaking out of the room while the pale-faced man's back was turned and never coming back. But I didn't. Of course I didn't.

"What are you going to say?" said the pale-faced man, after he had explained how to operate the telephones and computers that were the tools of the telephone interviewing trade. "What are you going to say when someone tells you they don't want to be interviewed? When they're 'too busy,' or when they're, 'just popping out,' or when they're, 'in the middle of something'?"

He waved his hands about and put on silly voices; he made it sound like everyone in the world was a rotten liar.

I noticed that his clothes were covered in a variety of stains. It didn't look like he bothered to wash them too often.

A girl in the front row raised her hand, keen to make a good impression.

"Yes, my love," said the pale-faced man.

"Could you just, sort of, tell them it will only take a couple of minutes?" the girl asked naively, with unforgivable enthusiasm.

"But it's going to take at least five minutes," said the pale-faced man. "You can't lie to the consumers."

That was what they called people at the market research company; they called people 'consumers'. Unless, of course, you happened to work for the market research company, in which case you were called a 'telephone interviewer'. Everyone was something or other; the market research company had a name for everyone.

The pale-faced man smiled a sickly smile at the girl in the front row, as if to suggest that he didn't think any less of her for having given such a foolish answer.

"Anyone else?" he said.

I wanted to raise my hand and say something funny and clever that would make him look silly, but I couldn't think of anything sufficiently funny and clever to say.

A spotty boy with immaculately combed hair raised his hand. "What about just saying, 'It will only take five minutes or so,' if it will only take five minutes or so? That doesn't sound too unreas-," he said.

"No! Sorry, I'm busy," said the pale-faced man, interrupting the spotty boy, and slamming his clenched fist on the desk in front of him to represent the 'consumer' slamming the receiver of his or her phone down, and thus dashing all hopes of a successful telephone interview being conducted.

The pale-faced man stared at the spotty boy with neat hair, as if he had just jeopardised, by his outright idiocy, the livelihoods of everyone who relied on the market research company for their livelihood.

The spotty boy wilted under his disdainful stare though his hair remained immaculately combed.

"Well," said the spotty boy, clearly not knowing what to say, but wanting to say something, to at least try and redeem himself, even if the attempt was futile. "You can't force someone to take part."

The pale-faced man looked at him scornfully, as if forcing someone to take part was exactly what you could do, and the spotty boy was a fool for suggesting otherwise.

"You never, ev-er accept that someone is too busy to spare the time to take part in an interview," he said trying to sound incredibly serious, like interviewing people on the telephone was an incredibly serious business that must, at all times and without exception, be taken incredibly seriously.

"You never, ev-er accept that someone is too busy to spare the time to take part in an interview, or you're out!" he said, as if conducting telephone interviews was really a matter of life or death.

He paused for dramatic effect.

(Pause)

The pale-faced man seemed incredibly satisfied with this little piece of oratory, which he had probably performed about ten thousand times before, and smiled to himself smugly as he paced to and fro at the front of the room.

He sighed deeply.

"Does anyone have any idea what to say when someone tells you they're busy?" he asked. Of course, no one volunteered to say anything at all.

I wanted to put my hand up and say something funny and clever that would render the pale-faced man speechless, and make the spotty boy laugh, and make the girl in the front row think I was funny and clever, but I couldn't think of anything appropriately funny and clever to say, so I didn't put my hand up and I said nothing.

The pale-faced man looked satisfied. He had established beyond doubt that he was the only person in the room who had a clue what he was going to say.

"Well, let me tell you what to say," he said, looking pleased with himself and wagging his finger. "Works every time."

The First Night of My Brother's Stag Trip

It was on my brother's stag trip that it happened. The summer was almost over.

Soon I would be trying not to draw attention to myself, and it would be time to get a job at the pie factory.

My brother was getting married. He had managed to convince someone to marry him. I'm not sure how. He never told me and I never asked.

His stag trip consisted of about eight men cruising up and down a river on a barge for an entire weekend. In those days that was the kind of thing a man was expected to do before he got married: he was expected to cruise up and down a river on a barge, or something like that, with about eight other men for an entire weekend.

And he was expected to invite his brother, even if he didn't particularly like his brother.

So that is what he did.

My brother and his friends were the kind of people who gave each other nicknames, and often talked about what a good bloke so-and-so or so-and-so was, and you couldn't really join in with the conversation if you didn't know who so-and-so or so-and-so was.

I think it's fair to say that I didn't really get on that well with my brother's friends. We had a sort of mutual understanding: I didn't like them and they didn't like me. I'm not really sure why. It's just the way it was.

I can only remember two of my brother's friends with any clarity at all. They were known as Ratty and The Undertaker, or at least I knew them as Ratty and The Undertaker.

When I close my eyes I can still see their faces in my mind.

The others are just blurry indistinct smudges, and when I close my eyes all I can see are blurry indistinct smudges.

Ratty was so called because he carried diseases. The diseases he carried were, or so he liked to boast, sexual in nature, and indicated an active sex life, if not a healthy one. From the moment I met him I thought him a grotesque human being; but I had to admit that other people seemed to like him well enough. I had no idea why.

He was the sort of person that might be described as 'larger than life'. I don't know about you but, personally, I've never thought that to be a good thing.

If you want to imagine what he looked like, he was below average height, above average weight, and had a short but tousled hairstyle. His cheeks were chubby and he had a kind of baby face; but make no mistake, it was a vulgar, grotesque baby.

The Undertaker was so called because his father was an undertaker. He was being primed to take over the family business and claimed to have seen more dead bodies than living ones. The Undertaker liked to mention dead bodies at any opportunity.

He seemed to possess a natural authority, which meant that when he spoke people listened; he was rarely questioned or contradicted. I guess you try not to argue with a guy who buries people for a living. But somehow he managed to be grave and affable at the same time. I'm not sure how he managed it, but he did.

He was the only one on that trip who ever tried to initiate a conversation with me.

He asked me what I wanted to do with my life.

I told him I wanted to be an astronaut. I didn't. It just seemed like a funny thing to say.

He laughed. He knew I didn't really mean it. He knew it was meant to be a joke. There was no way on earth that I was ever going to be an astronaut. He thought I was dead funny, or at least he acted as though he did.

As well as being grave and affable, The Undertaker had one hell of a sense of humour, which was as dry as a desiccated corpse.

The first night of my brother's stag trip was horrible. It just wasn't pleasant in any way at all, at least not for me. For me it was horrible from start to finish. In fact, every night of the stag trip was horrible, but let's deal with the first night first. That does at least seem logical.

We had picked up the boat in the afternoon. I hardly spoke a word to anyone, apart from The Undertaker who asked me what I wanted to do with my life, and who I told that I wanted to be an astronaut.

We drifted downriver until the sun began to slowly disappear behind some trees in the distance. Then the night began: the first horrible night of my brother's stag trip.

We moored at a quaint riverside village and I followed my brother and his friends as they looked for somewhere to get drunk, which is what they were expected to do.

I felt like a ghost. People kept bumping into me; I wondered if they could see me or not.

It didn't take them too long to find somewhere to get drunk; finding somewhere to get drunk is never too difficult. They ordered their drinks and settled down to get drunk and make each other laugh. It hardly seems worth mentioning that they succeeded on both counts, without too much trouble.

I tried to get drunk too. I thought it might help.

It didn't.

I tried to join in, I really did. At least a couple of times I thought of something to say that I thought might be quite amusing, but each time there was a slight pause in the conversation, and I started to speak, someone else started talking as well, and no one paid me any attention. It was as if they couldn't hear me. They just carried on saying the things that they had thought of to say without stopping to listen to what I had thought of to say. Naturally, this discouraged me and I quickly lost heart.

I felt like a ghost; I wondered if they could even hear me or not.

Their banter became more arcane as the evening progressed. The conversation was a labyrinth of inanely intricate private jokes: words whose connotations I did not understand, symbols whose meaning I could not fathom.

The waves of their laughter crashed against me, eroding me; I was tossed about like a baby in a boat.

I began to feel incredibly awkward and self-conscious because I didn't understand why things were so funny, and I hadn't said anything for what felt like hours and hours and hours.

My brother and his friends were really good at ignoring me. It seemed to come naturally to them. They acted as though I wasn't there without any effort at all.

The awkwardness became unbearable so I went to the toilet to relieve my discomfort. I got up without a word. I desperately needed the comfort of a few moments of solitude.

I locked myself in a cubicle and eked out the moments of solitude for as long as I could. But there's only so long you can spend in a cubicle, eking out moments of solitude, and it's not very long.

I made my way back to my brother and his friends as slowly as possible, but when I returned to the table where we had been sitting they were gone. Only their empty glasses remained, left behind as monuments to the drinks they had drunk and the laughter they had shared.

They were nowhere to be seen. They were gone. Perhaps they hadn't noticed that I wasn't there. After all, pretending that I wasn't there had seemed to come pretty naturally to them.

'Oh, shit,' I thought. 'What am I going to do now?' I had no idea what to do with myself. No idea at all.

I looked around to see if anyone had noticed my humiliation, but it didn't look like anyone had, which was a relief.

I turned around and walked out of the pub, as if turning around and walking out of the pub at that precise moment had always been part of the plan.

Outside, the quaint riverside village was exactly as still and quiet as you would expect, however still and quiet that may be.

I imagined that the men I was with had returned to the barge to carry on drinking, and so I wandered around for a while, trying to delay my return to the boat for as long as possible, trying to eke out the precious moments of solitude for as long as I could.

I imagined that I was the last person alive on the entire planet and had the place to myself.

I imagined that everyone else had died or gone missing, or something.

But I couldn't delay my return to the boat forever.

When I eventually returned, the boat was quiet and all around was dead still.

I wondered if my brother and his friends were already on the boat, or whether they had not yet returned. It was impossible to tell.

The door of the boat was locked so I lay down on the roof. I looked up at the stars. They seemed cold and distant; they were too far away to offer me any comfort at all.

I felt like a ghost, haunting myself.

Nothing happened, and I was tired, so I fell asleep.

It felt like only minutes later when I was woken by the sound of drunken men laughing and talking raucously. It felt like only minutes, but it may well have been hours. I couldn't be sure.

The drunken men were my brother's friends. Obviously.

The drunken men had no concern for anyone who might be trying to sleep, even though it was late at night and people might be trying to sleep. They were drunken men on a stag trip and no one would expect them to have any concern for people who might be trying to sleep.

I didn't want the drunken men to notice me lying on the roof of the boat, so I closed my eyes. For some reason, I thought that closing my eyes would make them less likely to notice me, and so I closed my eyes as tightly as I could.

But to no avail: despite the fact that my eyes were tightly shut, the drunken men still noticed me.

Ratty was the first to see me there, sleeping on the roof of the boat; he suggested playing some sort of 'joke' on me, such as tying me up, or removing my clothes and throwing them in the river. I wondered whether it was Ratty who had suggested abandoning me at the pub; he was a funny guy.

But The Undertaker was having none of it.

"Oh, grow up for fuck's sake. Leave the poor bastard alone," he said, in his grave and authoritative tones.

Ratty backed down. Like I said, you don't argue with a guy who buries dead bodies for a living.

The drunken men clumsily disappeared inside the boat. I heard them clumsily knocking about below me, and then the quietness and the stillness of the quaint riverside village returned. I decided I would wait until they were definitely asleep, and then creep into the boat and sleep in the relative comfort of the bunks inside. However, before I could be certain that they were definitely asleep, I fell asleep myself.

If felt like only minutes later when I was woken again, this time by the sound of urgent hurried fucking that was taking place on the towpath only feet away from my head.

One of the people fucking was my brother; I recognised his voice.

I turned my head slowly and, peeking through narrow slits – I didn't dare open my eyes fully for fear of giving myself away - I could see my brother fucking a girl from behind. In the bruised light of predawn their flesh looked pale and ghostly.

"Ugghhh! Ugghhh! Ugghhh!" grunted my brother rhythmically.

"Ahhh! Ooohhh! Ahhh!" moaned a female voice, but it was hard to tell if it was moaning in pleasure, or was just being polite. The moaning sounded strained, somehow.

My brother was standing up, while the girl was leaning over using a bench for support; his legs were hairless and deathly and his trousers were bunched at his ankles.

The grunting and moaning was becoming faster, more climactic.

"Uggghhhh! Ugggghhhhh! Uggggghhhhhh! Oooh! Ooooh! Oooooh! Ooooooh! Oooooooh! Ooooooooh! Aaaggghhhh! Aaaagggghhhhh!" said my brother.

"Ahhh! Ahhhh! Oooooh! Ahhhhhh!" said the girl.

The slapping sound of pale ghostly flesh on pale ghostly flesh suddenly stopped. My brother shuddered and chugged like a train reaching the end of the line.

"Oohh! Ooohhh! Oooohhhh! Fuuuck!" he said.

"Oh," said the girl.

There was a moment of climactic silence.

"Fuck me," my brother said. He was the kind of person who felt it necessary to fill silences. He was that kind of person.

He sat down on the bench, and stroked the girl's thighs as she pulled up her tights. "That was fucking great," he said.

"Hmmm," said the girl, as if trying to avoid being contrary or dishonest. She seemed nice enough. She straightened herself out. "Right. I've got to go," she said, without ceremony. I didn't blame her for wanting to leave at the first opportunity. I would have done the same, but I had nowhere to go. If I had had somewhere to go, I definitely would have done the same.

"See you later," she said, and left.

"Bye then," said my brother. And that was it; she was gone. I watched my brother watch her walk away.

When he had finished watching her walk away my brother stood up and hobbled towards the boat. I quickly shut my eyes as tightly as I could, but it was no use.

"Fucking hell!" he said to himself incredulously, noticing me. "What a dick." He clambered onto the boat and clumsily disappeared inside. I heard him lock the door, locking me out.

He knocked about noisily just below me, and then the quietness and the stillness of the quaint riverside village reasserted itself.

I shut my eyes tightly against the encroaching day but sleep did not come easy. I looked up at the sky, but it was cold and distant, and offered me no comfort at all. I closed my eyes again, but then became too acutely aware of the vast emptiness above me, and it is hard to sleep when you are too acutely aware of a vast emptiness above you. I must have eventually dropped off, however, because when I awoke the morning sun was burning me insidiously. It was going to be a hot day.

I was sore and stiff from a night lying on the roof of the boat.

I wished that I was somewhere else.

But I wasn't and wishing did me no good at all.

The New Moisturising Anti-Bacterial Soap Brand

Having completed my training, I was expected to conduct telephone interviews with unsuspecting members of the public: the 'consumers'. It was inevitable that, having completed my training, I would then be expected to conduct telephone interviews with the 'consumers'. There was no getting round it.

The pale-faced man showed me to my workstation. "Here's your workstation," he said, as if he had about a million other things to do. "There's your phone," he continued. "Important that." He winked at me. He sure was witty. "And that is your computer. Press that to get started." He pressed that. A telephone number and a name appeared on the black screen in green computer writing.

"OK, there you go. Have fun," he said.

The pale-faced man smiled at me insincerely and never spoke to me again. I was no longer his concern. My training was complete.

He nodded slightly at another employee of the market research company - who was sat at the head of the row of workstations - as if handing over responsibility.

The pale-faced man walked away and soon disappeared out of sight. I don't think I ever saw him again; or, at least, I don't remember ever seeing him again. Maybe I saw him once or twice rushing about in the distance, but if I did I have no memory of it.

The person whose concern I now was was a woman, but I didn't realise straight away. At first, for some reason, I thought she was a man.

She had dark greasy hair and wore a stern expression.

I realised she was staring at me: a stony, pitiless stare. I wondered what it would feel like to be turned to stone. Probably not too great, I imagined.

She was wearing headphones and I later discovered that she was listening to the 'telephone interviewers' under her command; she was listening to the 'telephone interviewers' conducting – or attempting to conduct – telephone interviews, and making sure they did it properly, to her satisfaction.

The 'telephone interviewers' were arranged in rows with workstations facing each other across a partition, which meant that all you could see of the person opposite you was a stray wisp of hair, or a suggestion of forehead, or occasionally a hint of ear or eyebrow. There were also partitions between each workstation so that even to see the person sitting next to you, you had to lean right back in your chair and crane your neck, which wasn't an easy position to maintain for too long.

Someone wearing headphones supervised each row. They were called the 'supervisors'. They over saw. Or over heard.

There was a wisp of hair opposite me that belonged to a girl who was in the middle of conducting a telephone interview. The stern woman was listening to her intently. So was I. And the sound of her voice and the wisp of hair were enough to make me imagine I had fallen in love.

And, from that moment on, I imagined that I had fallen in love with the girl opposite me: the girl with the wisp of hair.

"OK," she said, and my heart ached, "and how often would you say you use the new moisturising anti-bacterial soap brand's products? Every day, um, three or four times a week, two or three times a week, once a week, um, or ... less often?"

It sounded like she didn't really know what she was doing. She was hesitant, which only served to make my heartache more acute.

"Oh, I'm sorry, um, if you could just give me a minute ... um ..." she said.

"If you could just hold on a minute," said the girl with the wisp of hair, starting to sound slightly panicked.

I later realised that she had hit the button that terminated the interview rather than the button that progressed onto the next question. The girl with the wisp of hair was left stranded, without any questions to ask and only a blank screen for guidance. It was an easy mistake to make. It wouldn't be too long before I would be making the same mistake myself.

The stern woman's expression darkened. I guessed she wasn't too happy, but it was hard to tell because she never looked too happy. Perhaps being stern made her happy but it was hard to tell. She pressed the headphones she was wearing to her ears, while staring with an almost psychopathic intensity at the computer screen in front of her.

"I'm, um, having some ... technical, um, difficulties. Could I call you back in a few minutes," said the girl with the wisp of hair.

But it was too late. The 'consumer' had lost patience and hung up the phone. That's the thing with 'consumers': the thing with 'consumers' is that before too long they lose patience and hang up the phone.

The stern woman sighed impatiently. "Come here, please," she said, pitilessly, to the girl with the wisp of hair, making no allowances for the fact that the sight of a wisp of her hair and the sound of her voice was enough to make a person imagine they had fallen in love.

The girl with the wisp of hair stood up and suddenly she was more than just a wisp of hair and a voice that made my heart ache. She was also a body and a face that made my heart ache.

She walked a few paces and stood by the side of the stern woman.

"I know you're new," said the stern woman, "but let's face it, it's not difficult is it? I mean, we're not asking you to send a man into space, or perform open-heart surgery, are we?" she said sarcastically, as if sending a man into space, or performing open-heart surgery were the only difficult things a person could do, as if conducting telephone interviews wasn't, in its own way, also a difficult thing to do. "You press the button on the right to progress to the next question; you press the space bar to terminate the interview. We could train monkeys to do this."

She turned sternly away as if she couldn't bear to look at the girl with the wisp of hair's stupid face any longer; then, after a pause, looked back at her as if it cost her a great effort to do so.

"This is your last warning. OK? If this happens again, you're out," she said.

"OK," said the girl with the wisp of hair. "Can I go and sit back down now?" she said, as if unaccustomed to being spoken to so rudely, which she probably was. Most people probably made allowances for the fact that the sight of a wisp of her hair and the sound of her voice was enough to make a person imagine they had fallen in love.

I watched her as she returned to her seat and imagined that I had fallen in love.

GETTING TO KNOW THE GIRL WITH THE WISP OF HAIR

I got to know the girl with the wisp of hair in the 'smoking room' that the market research company provided for its employees to smoke in.

The 'smoking room' was what they called a yellowing cubicle that might once have been used as a stationery cupboard before it had been designated as a 'smoking room' for the employees of the market research company to smoke in. Inside, the smoke hung in the air like a rain cloud with nowhere to go.

She was easy to listen to. It was like lying on a freshly made bed in a sunlit room that was miles away from anywhere, and listening to the sounds that the world makes when it has nothing in particular to do. It was no effort at all.

She told me that she was from a small village that I wouldn't have heard of.

Her father was a priest of some sort, and expected her to adhere to a strict moral code of his own devising. I can't remember what sort of priest he was, and if she ever told me I have forgotten.

While her father preached and moralised, her mother kept herself busy by being an alcoholic, which kept her very busy indeed. Her father pretended not to notice how busy his wife was; he pretended not to notice a lot of things if the girl with the wisp of hair was to be believed, which I think she was.

The girl with the wisp of hair hated the small village that I wouldn't have heard of and couldn't get out of there fast enough.

And she was glad she left, even if it meant working in a crumby place like the market research company with crumby jerks like the stern woman.

Anything was better than living in the small village that you wouldn't have heard of with her father the priest and her mother the alcoholic.

At least that is what I remember her telling me; although, it is at least possible that I got it all muddled up with a movie I saw or a book I read. I can't be too sure.

The Invitation to My Brother's Second Wedding

I don't remember my brother's first wedding.
I don't remember my brother's first wedding because I didn't attend my brother's first wedding. It's as simple as that.

At the time I was trying not to draw attention to myself, and believed, quite rightly, that attending my brother's wedding would compromise my efforts. So I stayed at home, where I was better able not to draw attention to myself.

I don't remember my brother's first wedding but I remember his second. I'll remember his second for as long as I draw breath. It will probably be the last thing I remember before I die.

By the time of his second wedding my brother was a rich man, which was all he had ever wanted to be. He had set out to be rich, and he had succeeded. He was a rich and successful man.

I hadn't really known his first wife very well. I met her once or twice, as you know, but I never really got to know her very well, or at all, to tell the truth. I'm not even sure I ever spoke to her other than to say hello and goodbye, or yes please or no thank you. And I've no idea why their marriage fell apart. I've no idea why marriages fall apart in general. I imagine that people just get sick of seeing each other, and hearing each other, and smelling each other, and touching each other, and decide that they want to start seeing, hearing, smelling and touching someone else. I guess that's how it works.

I imagine that my brother probably felt that a rich and successful man like himself deserved a new wife just as he might have deserved a new car, or clean underwear. Maybe he thought a rich and successful man like himself was expected to find a new wife; maybe he was just doing what he thought was expected of him.

By the time the invitation to my brother's second wedding arrived in the post, I had lost count of the number of years I had not spoken to him for. I hadn't been counting, but it was a very long time; it was long enough to feel like a lifetime, which is a thing people say, even though very few people actually know what a lifetime feels like.

But despite the fact that we hadn't spoken for quite a considerable number of years, and despite the fact that neither of us felt any affection towards the other, he still invited me to his second wedding. After all, people are expected to invite their brothers to their weddings, even if they think their brothers are a complete waste of space. If you're not going to invite your brother to your wedding, then you better have a damn good reason, and just thinking that your brother's a waste of space isn't really a good enough reason.

The invitation was lucky to find me. If I had moved in the years since my brother and I had last spoken, it would probably not have found me at all. Mother was long dead, as was father, and apart from the fact that we were brothers, there were no other ties connecting us.

But I hadn't moved. I had stayed exactly where I was, and so the invitation found me without too much trouble at all.

The Invitation to My Brother's Second Wedding (Continued)

I hate it when people personify things. It really annoys me. Like when a book says, 'Open me'. I can't think of many things more annoying than that.

It would not be an exaggeration to say that I was shocked to receive an invitation to my brother's second wedding. I was shocked. I sat in stunned silence for several minutes after opening the invitation. I didn't move for several minutes but just stared at the invitation I had received in dumb horror. There was something terrifying about it that rendered me motionless.

While I sat there staring in shock at the invitation I had just received, I realised that before receiving the invitation I had not spoken to my brother for so many years that I had begun to wonder whether he was even still alive. Not that it mattered. When you haven't seen or spoken to someone for as many years as I had not seen or spoken to my brother – however many years that may have been – it doesn't really matter whether they are alive or dead, or anywhere in between. It doesn't really matter at all until they send you an invitation to their second wedding; and then it suddenly matters a great deal.

Receiving the invitation to my brother's second wedding banished all doubts: he was definitely still alive, and was even getting married again, as if to prove it to the world.

I stared at the invitation in dumb horror. The invitation terrified me and I certainly considered never looking at it again.

I was unemployed and had been for quite a number of years. I was living the barest of existences. I had no money and ate frugally; I wore the same threadbare, ill-fitting clothes every day. I never spoke to anyone.

This made attending my brother's second wedding fraught with difficulty. For a start I would need to buy myself a suit. I would also need to pay for transport, drinks, accommodation, none of which I could afford, or come anywhere near affording. Unlike my brother, I was not rich or successful. I was poor. And a miserable failure.

The only thing I had ever been good at was not drawing attention to myself. I was good at that. I was certainly not a miserable failure when it came to not drawing attention to myself.

And I hadn't had a conversation in years. Not a proper conversation anyway. The local shopkeeper asked me how I was occasionally, but he didn't really care. He was the human being that I saw most often in the world, but he didn't really care how I was. And, really, it was too much to expect him to. I had given him absolutely no reason to care how I was and, if I'm honest with myself - which I try to be - I didn't care how he was either.

Once, when he asked me how I was, I told him that I wasn't so good. "Not so good, I'm afraid," I might have said, or something like that. But the local shopkeeper asked no follow-up questions; he just acted as though I had told him I was fine, and didn't ask a single follow-up question.

I wonder if you know, or can imagine, what it's like to not have a proper conversation with anyone for a number of years.

Not that I want you to feel sorry for me. I don't. Don't feel sorry for me.

It's not too bad, actually. You get used to it, and you manage to convince yourself that it's not too bad, and that you'd be quite happy to never have a proper conversation with anyone ever again.

Until, that is, you receive an invitation to attend your brother's second wedding, and then the fact that you have received an invitation to attend your brother's second wedding sends you into fits of anxiety, because you haven't had a proper conversation with anyone for a number of years, and you imagine that, if you ever had the ability to sustain a conversation with another human being, then surely, through years of neglect, that ability has been lost.

It's perfectly obvious to me now that I should have declined the invitation but, for some reason, I felt an odd inexplicable determination to attend the wedding. Against my better judgement, which I have to admit, didn't amount to much, I was determined to accept the invitation.

To this day, I'm not really sure why.

Perhaps I was curious to see how he had changed in the years since I had last seen him.

Perhaps I wanted an excuse to buy a new suit. Perhaps I knew that without an excuse to buy a new suit, I would never buy a new suit again.

Perhaps I wanted to have a proper conversation with someone. Perhaps I knew ...

Perhaps.

I'm not really sure.

Not Telephone Interviewing

I wasn't much good at telephone interviewing to tell the truth. I was ill-suited to the line of work.

I just didn't like pestering people. Whenever I managed to get through my introductory speech, which wasn't too often, they just sounded fed up, like they had a million other things to do and the last thing they needed was to be pestered. And I couldn't blame them; no one likes being pestered. Being pestered is just not a thing people like.

At the end of my first shift, which had lasted for several consecutive hours, I had not conducted a single telephone interview. Not even one. I hadn't even had a sniff of interest in telephone interviews.

At the end of my first shift the stern woman summoned me to her desk.

"No interviews," she said sternly, as if we both knew how serious it was. She looked at me intently as if expecting some sort of explanation. I offered none and she looked a little disappointed.

"OK," she said, having realised that no explanation was forthcoming. "It's not good enough. If you want to work here you are going to have to be more assertive," she said, enunciating each word very precisely like a psychopath in a movie.

"You tell them anything to get them to do the interview. OK. A-ny-thing. Tell them it will only take a few minutes; tell them it's a unique opportunity to get their voice heard; tell them your life depends on it if you have to."

I was beginning to think it might.

Little compact balls of spit flew from her mouth. They landed on the desk in front of her, maintaining their shape for a few seconds before collapsing into tiny little puddles of spittle. "I don't care what you say, just get the interviews done," she said, sternly.

"I'll do my best," I said, because I couldn't think of anything else to say.

"You better," she said, and it sounded like a threat. It sounded like if I didn't do my best she would beat me half to death with a heavy stick or something. "Another day like today and you're out. OK?"

"OK."

"And that's your last warning."

It was also my first warning, but that was just how things worked at the market research company. Every warning was your last warning; it was just the way it worked.

"OK," I said, not wanting to say more than was strictly necessary.

There was a momentary silence that she filled with sternness. She shooed me away, like an ugly cat.

The Invitation Speaks

The invitation to my brother's second wedding sat on the table in front of me. It looked at me. It was a questioning look; it was a challenging look. It was a look that wasn't going to back down.

"So," it said, "are you going to attend your brother's second wedding or not?"

I had been having second thoughts. "I'm not sure," I said.

It was not unusual for me to talk to things that would never talk back, so I wasn't too surprised to find myself talking to a wedding invitation.

"You've got no good reason not to, have you?" it said. "After all, what kind of person would even think about not going to their brother's wedding?" The invitation was questioning me in what seemed like an unnecessarily confrontational manner.

"I've got my reasons," I said defensively. "For starters, he hasn't contacted me in years."

"And you haven't contacted him! You should be pleased he invited you," the invitation said.

"But I don't have a suit," I said. I knew the invitation would have an answer ready.

"Oh, come on! You're just making excuses now. Steal one for god's sake! You've no compunction in that department."

That invitation knew me pretty well. I was not above stealing things. I had been doing it for years. Not big things, of course, but little things, like ham and cheese and things like that, when I fancied a treat.

"But it's been so long since I had a proper conversation with anyone. I'm not even sure I can do it anymore. I'm not sure I can ever do it again," I said, beginning to sound petulant, wilting under the invitation's interrogation.

"So, you're happy to never speak to anyone ever again, are you? You're just going to sit here, on your own, day in day out until you die, never speaking to anyone apart the local shopkeeper who doesn't even care how you are!"

That invitation always knew what to say. Argument was futile. It was a smart invitation. It always had an answer ready. It was that kind of invitation: the kind of invitation that always has an answer ready.

The invitation knew it had won the argument.

"So, are you going to go or what?"

"OK, OK. I'll go, I'll go," I said, even though I knew I was speaking to an invitation.

The invitation slouched smugly on the table in front of me. I picked it up and held it in my hands, staring at it in disbelief. It looked exactly like you would expect a wedding invitation to look.

It was written in a formal, almost solemn style in an ornate decorative font, as you would expect. Floral patterns framed the writing. They were golden and shiny and protruded slightly from the brilliantly white card. I ran my finger over the intricate floral pattern. It felt nice.

"Hey! Hands off!" it said aggressively.

"You'd better go," it added, with more than a hint of malice.

The invitation had somehow convinced me that I didn't really have a choice.

I sighed. "All right, I'll go," I said, even though there was no other human being in the room, and many good reasons not to. "I'll go."

Days

Days progressed in a similar manner for several days, which is something that days tend to do if you're not careful.

Days: workstation, telephone, computer, wisp of hair, green computer writing, the stern woman, no telephone interviews, last warnings, etc.

The market research company.

I tried, mostly unsuccessfully, to conduct telephone interviews. I was given more last warnings, and each last warning seemed to make a mockery of the previous last warning, which in its turn had made a mockery of the last warning before that.

But, somehow, I seemed to manage to secure enough answers to questions to make my occupation of a workstation tenable, for the time being at least.

On occasion, when our breaks coincided, I listened to the girl with the wisp of hair talk as we sat in the 'smoking room' smoking. She was easy to listen to; it was no effort at all.

She told me that her little brother died when she was eight. He fell headfirst down a well; he had been making a wish. She didn't tell me how he fell headfirst into the well and I didn't ask.

I wondered how a little brother could fall headfirst into a well. Perhaps he leaned too far over the edge.

She was the kind of person whose father was some sort of priest and whose little brother fell headfirst down a well. That is unless I have got it all mixed up with some movie I saw or book I read. She may not have been that kind of person at all.

Following the Girl with the Wisp of Hair

One day I came in late and received a last warning for doing so.

"You're late," the stern woman told me, unnecessarily. We both knew that I was late. It was obvious.

"Is everything OK?" she asked me, not unreasonably. Often, I suppose, people are late to work because everything is not OK; maybe they left the gas on, or their car broke down, or their kid got sick, or something like that.

"Everything's fine," I said, sticking to my rule of not saying more to the stern woman than was strictly necessary.

"Look," said the stern woman, getting down to business. She leaned forward to let me know it was time to get down to business, and that she was getting down to business. "You can't carry on like this. This is it now. This is your final warning. One more slip up and you're out. Finished. You can't go on like this."

I wondered if a 'final' warning was different to a 'last' warning. I decided that it was: a final warning was much more serious.

"OK," I said, which was the minimum I could get away with saying.

I sat down at my workstation and lost myself in the wisp of hair and the sweet voice opposite until it was time to go home.

Our shifts finished at the same time. I desperately wanted to ask her to go for a drink or something, but she left in a hurry before I had a chance to ask her. She seemed to be in a hurry for some reason.

Then, without having consciously decided that I was going to do any such thing, I started following her.

I followed her down the rank alleyway that led to the main road.

I followed her as she rushed through the streets.

I stopped and watched from across the street as she disappeared inside a shop, and carried on watching as she emerged with a brand new packet of cigarettes, and opened the brand new packet of cigarettes, and took out a brand new cigarette, and began smoking it as she continued rushing through the busy streets.

I followed her as she rushed through the busy streets.

I watched as she crashed into an old man and almost sent him flying. 'Busy streets are really no place for old men,' I thought. 'Busy streets are a young person's game.' She apologised to the old man and continued rushing through the busy streets.

I didn't stop following her as she rushed through the busy streets. I kept right on following her.

She rushed into the train station, which if seen from above might have resembled an ants' nest, or a beehive, or something like that. I followed her into the train station, wondering why she was in such a rush.

I watched, trying to look inconspicuous, as she made a call on a public telephone, looking anxiously left and right as she did so. I wondered who she was speaking to in such a rush.

I followed her as she rushed to the platform. I watched her tap her foot and check the clock, and pace up and down, and rummage about in her bag, and look impatient, and I wondered why she seemed so impatient.

I kept a safe distance and was pretty confident that she had no idea I was following her.

The train arrived and the girl with the wisp of hair hurriedly boarded, as if she thought that her hurrying might hurry the train along also, which seemed unlikely. I boarded the train too, because without having consciously decided to, I was following the girl with the wisp of hair.

I was trying to be discreet, so I didn't board the same coach as the girl with the wisp of hair, but boarded the next one along.

The train chugged out of the station because that's what trains do: they chug. Chug, chug, chug.

When it had finished chugging out of the station the train began rolling past houses and streets, which all belonged to someone or other, because that's just how it works: everything in this world belongs to someone or other. It has to; there's no other way.

The train wasn't able to build up too much speed because it soon had to stop at another station. As it neared the station, the train began chugging again until it ground to a halt.

I had no idea where the girl with the wisp of hair would disembark, so when the train stopped I pressed my face against the window and looked rapidly left and right to see if I could spot her on the platform. I couldn't. As far as I could tell she was still on the train, which soon began chugging its way out of the station.

"Chug, chug, chug," said the train, as if it wasn't too thrilled at the prospect of having to start chugging again, as if all this chugging was really a bit of a nuisance, and it would far rather just not chug at all. I felt for that train, I really did. I felt like we understood each other.

Once the train was rolling again, its smooth motion punctuated by regular clanks and clangs, a ticket conductor started working his way down the carriage towards me.

"Tickets please," he kept saying as if he had said 'tickets please' about a million times before, and wanted nothing more than to never have to say 'tickets please' ever again.

With surprising speed he worked his way to me. I thought it would take him forever to work his way to me, but it didn't. The ticket conductor worked with ruthless efficiency.

I should probably have moved because I knew that I didn't have a ticket, but for some reason I didn't move. I stayed exactly where I was.

"Tickets please," he said, inevitably, to the world in general, which included me.

A couple of people presented their tickets like people who knew they possessed valid tickets, and therefore knew they had absolutely nothing to worry about. They wanted their tickets to be inspected. 'Look at me,' they seemed to be saying, 'I've got a valid ticket and I want the world to know.'

Another person presented his ticket like a man who had presented a valid ticket about a thousand million times before, and who expected to present about another thousand million valid tickets before he could retire from presenting valid tickets, and could think of nothing more mundane than the valid ticket he was presenting or the act of presenting it.

The ticket conductor turned his attention to me because I was the only person in the vicinity who had not presented a valid ticket.

I tried to act very much as if I had a valid ticket even though I knew full well that I had no such thing. I fumbled in a pocket and pulled out a tired receipt and some pocket fluff. I looked at the tired receipt and the pocket fluff, as if surprised that I had not produced a valid ticket.

I was pretty sure the ticket conductor, who had already sighed impatiently, could see through my whole act, but I kept going. I dug around in another pocket and my hand eventually emerged with a couple of copper coins and a button that was no good to anyone, and certainly wasn't a valid ticket. I looked at the button and the copper coins like a magician who couldn't quite understand why his trick hadn't worked.

"I must have lost it," I said. I patted myself down having run out of pockets to fumble in.

All the ticket conductor was interested in was whether I had a valid ticket or not. He wasn't interested in excuses or lies; he had heard them all about a thousand million times before.

He started writing something with a little pencil on a small notepad that he carried around in his pocket.

"You're going to have to pay a fine," he said, sounding almost relieved, as if telling me that I'd have to pay a fine was a welcome change from saying 'tickets please', which it probably was. "And you'll have to pay the full fare as well," he added.

He finished writing something with his little pencil on the small notepad that he carried around in his pocket for that purpose. He ripped the sheet from his notepad and handed it to me.

"Twenty-five pounds, please," he said, looking at me with eyes that had seen it all before. About a thousand million billion times.

The train began to chug again. "Chug, chug, chug," said the train.

"Come on," said the ticket conductor, as if he was talking to a small dirty child. "Twenty-five pounds, please."

I handed the ticket conductor the couple of copper coins and the button that was no good to anyone, and certainly wasn't a valid ticket. He wasn't too impressed.

"Look, you either pay the money or I take you to the police at the next station."

The train chugged to a halt. The doors of the carriage opened with an extended hiss. "Hisssssssssssssss," said the doors of the carriage.

I hadn't forgotten the reason I was there. I craned my neck to look down the platform. There she was! The girl with the wisp of hair! I enjoyed an obscured view of her rushing down the platform.

"Right, you're coming with me," said the ticket conductor, losing patience.

I got up quickly and brushed past him.

"Hey!" he said, his voice right behind me.

"It's all right," I told him as I rushed off the train, "I'm getting off here anyway."

But the ticket conductor knew how to deal with people like me. He had dealt with people like me about a thousand million times before. There wasn't a lot he hadn't seen before.

He grabbed me and pinned my hands behind my back with the masterful simplicity of someone who has performed a particular action about a million times before. He held me tightly and marched me towards a little office in the station.

There was a mass of rushing bodies on the platform, but in the distance I could easily pick out the girl with the wisp of hair; the girl from the small village that you wouldn't have heard of; the girl whose father was some sort of priest and whose little brother had fallen headfirst down a well when she was eight.

The girl with the wisp of hair: who I had imagined myself in love with, and who I saw for the last time as she rushed down the platform and disappeared into the crowd.

I wondered why she could possibly be in such a rush.

Small Island

It was the second day of my brother's stag trip, and it promised to be no better than the first.

You will remember that when I woke up the low morning sun was burning me insidiously, which wasn't a good start. I was sore and stiff from a night lying on the roof of the boat, which didn't help either.

I opened my eyes and wished, sincerely, that I was somewhere else. Somewhere else entirely. But I wasn't, and wishing did me no good at all.

The first thing I saw, once my eyes had adjusted to the brightness, was a blue sky above me that had no beginning and no end, and offered me no comfort whatsoever. Some people take some comfort from a blue sky, but not me. I took no comfort from it whatsoever.

The second thing I saw was local people walking their dogs on the towpath and looking at me disapprovingly.

I sat upright. I had no idea what time it was, but it felt like morning. There were no sounds from below, so I guessed that my brother and his friends were still asleep, which was fine by me.

I stood up and stretched which, for some reason, seemed to invite more vocal disapproval from the local people who were passing by. I was clearly not the kind of person they wanted to see in their local area as they walked their dogs in the morning. I couldn't really blame them. I'm just not the kind of person that people want to see in their local area as they walk their dogs in the morning. It's as simple as that.

I needed to relieve myself and so I hopped off the boat, almost falling over and making a fool of myself in the process. I was not too supple after a night sleeping on the roof of the boat. I went to find somewhere to relieve myself.

I must have been gone a while because when I returned The Undertaker was handing round bacon sandwiches.

"Ah, here he is," he said, noticing me. "We were beginning to think you'd fallen overboard!" The Undertaker smiled, but the others simply directed blank, vaguely hostile looks in my direction.

My brother looked at me as if to say, 'Actually, I wish you had fallen overboard, and I'm a little bit disappointed that you haven't.' Or at least that is what I thought he looked at me as if to say. I don't deny the possibility that I am doing him a disservice.

I remained standing mutely on the towpath. I had absolutely no idea what to say or do. One of my big problems in life is that I quite often have absolutely no idea what to say or do.

"You want some breakfast, mate?" The Undertaker asked me charitably. He was the kind of person who called everyone 'mate'. It didn't really mean anything; it wasn't a sign of affection or anything.

"No, I'm all right thanks. I've eaten," I said, but I hadn't eaten. I was lying. I was actually very hungry indeed. I had no idea why I was lying. It didn't make much sense. That's the thing with me: a lot of the time I'm my own worst enemy.

I made a decision that at the first opportunity I would sneak into the boat and eat a slice of bread or whatever else I could lay my hands on without anyone noticing.

"Are you sure, mate?" asked The Undertaker again, once I had stepped onto the roof of the boat. He was giving me another chance. He probably knew I was lying and that I hadn't already eaten, and that I was actually very hungry indeed. "There's plenty to go round."

"Yeah, no, I'm fine thanks," I said, unconvincingly.

"OK, suit yourself," said The Undertaker, as if he knew that I was actually very hungry indeed, but was, for some reason, pretending that I wasn't. Whether he knew or not, he decided against pressing the issue any further and disappeared purposefully inside the boat. The Undertaker was the kind of person who did everything purposefully.

My brother and the remainder of his friends – Ratty and the others - were sat around, ignoring me, eating bacon sandwiches, talking about the previous night.

"So, you fucked her then?" asked one of my brother's friends. I don't remember which. He was a blurry indistinct smudge, and will always remain so.

"Of course I fucking did," said my brother, as if offended that it had even been thought necessary to ask. "Fucked her right over there," he said, pointing. "Up the arse," he continued, while chewing on a bacon sandwich, little bits of bread and bacon spraying from his mouth. Some of his friends sniggered. He looked incredibly proud of himself; he was enjoying the attention.

"Dirty bitch," he added, as he ate. He was really struggling to contain the bits of bacon sandwich in his mouth.

At that moment the boat's engine grunted and spluttered into life and The Undertaker, who had taken the helm, shouted something that no one could hear over the noise.

The boat began moving ominously downriver.

My brother and his friends stayed outside talking loudly, so I ducked inside the boat and hastily ate a slice of bread without anyone noticing. I shoved the whole thing in my mouth at once. I think I would have died of shame and embarrassment if anyone had discovered me, but thankfully no one did.

We drifted downriver for endless hours that day; hour upon interminable hour, or so it seemed to me. To me it seemed as if the hours would never end.

My brother and his friends were having a great time, or seemed to be, and I imagine that for them the hours flew by. I imagine that whenever they looked at a clock or someone told them what time it was, they couldn't believe how quickly the time was flying by. 'Shit,' they might have said, 'is it that time already?'

I sat on the roof in the middle of the boat, as far away from everyone else as possible, and the hours seemed interminable. I wished I was somewhere else but it was no use. I remained stubbornly where I was.

At one point there was a sudden downpour that drove everyone inside the boat apart from The Undertaker who, as usual, was steering the boat, and myself. I decided pretty quickly as the rain began to fall that getting soaked was preferable to enduring the company of my brother and his friends in a confined space and having absolutely no idea what to say or do.

Anyway, it was a summer shower – if that's even a thing – and didn't last too long.

I got soaked, and though unpleasant, it was definitely preferable to the company of my brother and his friends and having no idea what to do or say.

We drifted downriver for hours; long, endless, interminable hours that never seemed to end, but just went on and on and on. I longed for some catastrophe to alleviate the tedium. But it was no use: catastrophe remained stubbornly elusive.

One of the things that my brother and his friends did to amuse themselves was shout insults at passers-by, or people who might be fishing or doing some other thing on the riverbank.

"Fucking paedophile!" Ratty shouted at a father fishing at the riverside with his son. The father stood up aggressively as if he wanted to avenge the insult that he had suffered, but soon realised that there was nothing he could do and so just stood there impotently. I almost felt sorry for him; after all, he was probably just trying to do something nice with his son. He didn't deserve to be insulted. Or at least I assumed he didn't.

They all laughed coarsely: Ratty, my brother, all of them. Even The Undertaker.

I felt like we had been drifting downriver for days when my brother began making his way cautiously along the side of the boat to join The Undertaker at the helm. There was no walkway along the side of the boat, only a little ledge that could be sidled along. And as my brother sidled cautiously along the little ledge, I thought about pushing him off and sending him crashing, humiliatingly, into the water. It would have been easy enough to do, and I could have claimed it was some sort of joke or something. It might even have helped my situation, which wasn't too great. But I didn't do it. Of course I didn't. It was just an idle thought and had no foothold in reality, like time travel or everything being all right in the end.

"What the fuck are you doing sitting here by yourself?" said my brother as he passed by. "You could at least try to act like a normal fucking person." He made no attempt to conceal his contempt.

I didn't reply.

"Fucking unbelievable. Ungrateful fuck," he said, as if speaking to no one in particular.

He soon reached the helm of the boat and began talking and laughing affably with The Undertaker. After a few minutes he pointed at something in the near distance and slapped The Undertaker on the back. The two men laughed heartily. The Undertaker seemed to be looking at me, but he was too far away for me to be sure. He cut the boat's engine. Its busy vibrations spluttered to a halt. There was a sort of calm as the water lapped against the gliding boat.

I looked ahead. The river had widened considerably and we were approaching a small island in the middle of the river. The island consisted of a few isolated tufts of grass, a couple of spindly trees and one or two bushes.

It was a small island and it really didn't have anything to recommend it.

We drifted towards the small island. I reluctantly became aware that The Undertaker was trying to attract my attention. I couldn't actually hear what he was saying but it was obvious he was trying to attract my attention.

I tried to ignore him, but he was terribly insistent and ignoring him didn't seem to have any effect.

"Yes," I said weakly in response to his insistent calls, even though I knew that there was no way he could possibly hear me. He beckoned me. I didn't move immediately, and so his gestures became more urgent and dramatic. He was steadfastly refusing to be ignored.

I rose to my feet and moved a little closer warily, as if approaching a wild animal. When I judged I was close enough to hear and be heard, I advanced no further. I didn't want to get closer than was absolutely necessary.

"Yes," I said, warily.

"We're going to moor here for a minute, mate. Can you jump off and grab the rope when I throw it to you?"

I guess I thought that when a person buries dead bodies for a living, it's best to do as he asks.

When the boat was near enough to the small island to jump ashore without getting wet, I jumped ashore. I was immensely relieved to land on the shore without getting wet or falling over. I was mightily relieved to have avoided that particular embarrassment. I actually thought it quite an achievement. I was almost pleased with myself.

I steadied myself ready to receive the rope from The Undertaker. But he didn't throw me a rope. Instead I heard the boat's engine growl belligerently back into life, and saw him steer hard away from the small island.

Before I had time to react the boat was several feet away from the shore. If I had reacted quickly enough I could probably have jumped back aboard without suffering too much shame. But I have never been one of those people who can react quickly to things. Things always seem to happen before I have time to react. Either I am always very slow to react, or things always happen very quickly. It's hard to tell which.

My brother laughed hysterically, as if me being stranded on a small island was the funniest thing that had ever happened.

"Sorry mate," shouted The Undertaker over the din of the engine. He sounded almost apologetic, or maybe I just imagined that he sounded almost apologetic. Maybe he didn't sound almost apologetic at all. "Sit tight, we'll be back later."

Ratty and the others hadn't realised what was happening straight away, but they soon did and their laughter joined with my brother's, and had a hollow sound as it bounced off the water.

I stood there like an idiot watching the boat drift slowly away and listening to the hollow sound of mocking laughter bouncing off the water. The boat became smaller and smaller until it disappeared round a bend.

I wondered anxiously what people would think if they saw me there, standing pointlessly on the small island. I looked around to see if anyone was watching me.

There was an old couple walking a dog on the riverbank opposite. They had a young boy with them, who I guessed was their grandson, not that it really matters. They had stopped walking and were watching me.

I didn't want them to think that I needed or wanted help, so I waved at them and casually sat down by one of the island's threadbare bushes as if sitting down by one of the island's threadbare bushes had been my plan all along.

Out of the corner of my eye I saw them shrug and walk on. The young boy who was with them kept looking back at me, the way that kids keep looking back at something that doesn't seem quite right.

I lay down, imagining that horizontal I would attract less attention than if I remained upright, which definitely seemed like a logical thing to imagine at the time.

Boats kept passing by and the people on the boats kept noticing me despite the fact that I was lying down and didn't want them to notice me. Men who combed their hair and wore unnecessary jumpers, which they draped over their shoulders so that it looked like their jumpers were hugging them, kept shouting at me, asking me if I was OK; some pointed me out to their friends.

'Look at that bloke there,' they might have said to their friends, 'lying on that small island. I wonder what the hell he's doing.'

'Weirdo,' their friends might have replied.

I ignored them all and tried to pretend that lying on the small island was what I had planned to do all along.

One boat came very near to the small island and its occupants called out to me to jump aboard, but I pretended to be asleep, so they gave up trying to save me and the boat just drifted on by.

It was the middle of the afternoon. It was the middle of a fine summer afternoon and the sun hung menacingly overhead.

I could feel myself burning, so after a while I sought what shelter the island's two spindly trees could provide, which was not a huge amount of shelter, it has to be said. In fact, it was hardly worth seeking at all. Nevertheless, I clung pathetically to the scant protection the two spindly trees provided, like a starving child gnawing at a stale scrap of bread.

I suppose I could have swum ashore. It wasn't too far and I was a reasonably strong swimmer. I could swim; I wouldn't have drowned.

Or I could have accepted one of the many offers of help.

Or I could have called out to one of the passing boats. 'Excuse me,' I could have said. 'I'm stuck on this small island. Could you help me?'

I could have done any of these things, but I didn't. I'm not really sure why.

Perhaps I didn't want to appear desperate.

Instead, I clung pathetically to the negligible shelter provided by the two spindly trees on the small island. I wasn't desperate; I was just pathetic: desperately pathetic.

'But,' I thought, 'if they don't come back for me soon I will have to do something.' I knew I couldn't stay there forever. Inaction, I knew, was only a temporary solution.

I decided that if my situation remained unchanged by evening I would swim to the riverbank and accept whatever might be waiting for me there.

But they came back. They came back for me.

The sky was purpling; the day had been beaten black and blue. My brother was still laughing, as if me being stranded on the small island was still the funniest thing that had ever happened.

I was slumped against one of the spindly trees in a daze. I felt strange. I made no effort to move but tried to look casual, as if, actually, it wasn't too bad being stranded all day on a small island with only a couple of spindly trees and a threadbare bush for company.

I must have felt pretty sick from being exposed to the sun all day, and must have cut a pretty woeful figure sitting there slumped against the spindly tree. The Undertaker threw a half empty bottle of water at me. It was an act of charity.

"Come on, mate," he said, as if no harm had been meant. "Drink that and get back on board." I imagined that there was a note of concern, but it might have been annoyance.

I still didn't move. My brother's laughter subsided and he frowned, as if angry with me for ceasing to amuse him.

I continued to not move.

"Get back on the fucking boat," my brother said, sounding pretty annoyed, as if I was doing my best to spoil his fun. "We haven't got all fucking day." He sounded drunk.

I got up slowly, with some difficulty. I was sore and stiff and probably badly sunburned. To tell the truth, I probably had sunstroke or some such thing. I felt a little dizzy and a little sick. I drank the half empty bottle of water and hoisted myself back onto the boat.

"Finally," said my brother sarcastically, like the massive bastard he was. "Fucking hell," he added unnecessarily.

I clambered shakily back on board and, without a word, resumed my position on the roof of the boat.

I wished I was somewhere else, but wishing did me no good at all.

Part Three

The Owner

I worked at the warehouse for a total of fifty-one weeks and apart from the delivery of hundreds of cheap pillows nothing remarkable happened.

At least not that I can remember.

Apart from the cheap pillows, pretty much everything else that got delivered arrived in square or rectangular boxes and could be stored neatly and efficiently.

I'm not sure if that's a metaphor for something, but it might be.

And because nothing remarkable had happened for so long, it felt like nothing remarkable would just keep happening for a long time to come.

But then, in the fifty-first week of my employment at the warehouse, something remarkable started happening.

It all started when the owner of the company pulled up at the warehouse in his shiny expensive-looking sports car. I had only ever seen the owner once before and that was when the company's accountant had been caught embezzling money. This was something the owner simply couldn't tolerate, because he needed that money to pay for his shiny expensive-looking sports car, and if the company's accountant was embezzling money it meant only one thing: less money for him. And he simply couldn't tolerate that.

He was dressed casually: he wore a shirt, but the top button was undone and he wasn't wearing a tie. He dressed like a man who could afford to dress casually. He dressed like a man who could dress smartly if he wanted without any trouble at all, but just chose not to. It was the look of a man who didn't answer to anyone.

I guessed that life had been kind to him because he drove a shiny expensive-looking sports car, and could afford to dress casually. But you never can tell for sure. Just because a man drives a shiny expensive-looking sports car, and can afford to dress casually, it doesn't necessarily follow that life has been kind to him. Terrible things can still happen to a man who drives a shiny expensive-looking sports car and can afford to dress casually.

'Something must be wrong,' I thought with pleasure. The owner only ever seemed to appear when things went wrong. I didn't have an awful lot of evidence to go on, but it definitely seemed to me that the owner only ever appeared when things went wrong.

The owner got out of his car and took a good look around. He was unhurried. He looked like the kind of man who didn't rush for anyone. He could afford not to rush for anyone. He was the owner. He didn't answer to anyone.

Taking one step at a time and not rushing for anyone, the owner climbed the exterior metallic skeletal staircase that led from the outside world to the office that was situated above the warehouse.

'I am the owner,' his gait suggested. 'And I don't rush for anyone.' At least that is what his gait seemed to suggest. But then, to tell the truth, I am no expert when it comes to interpreting a person's gait.

Later that day the employees of the company were called to the 'meeting room'. The 'meeting room' was where meetings took place. That's why they called it the 'meeting room', which was at least logical.

Having been summoned, I reluctantly made my way to the 'meeting room' and sat with the other employees of the company around an oblong table that was made of pretend wood. The table was made of a substance pretending to be wood. It wasn't doing too great a job but at least it was trying.

The owner sat at the head of the table leaning forward, his hands clasped in front of him. It was his table; he owned the table. He smiled benignly as if there was nothing in particular that was causing him undue concern.

Although physically unremarkable, when he spoke it was with a deep sonorous voice, which seemed to fill every inch of the room, or so it seemed to me. It was a voice that sounded like it held itself in high regard, and expected others to do likewise.

"Well, good afternoon everyone," said the owner, with a voice that filled every inch of the room. I also noticed that his skin was profoundly tanned, but I don't think it really matters.

He wore glasses too, if you're interested in stuff like whether people wear glasses or not.

"Now, as I'm sure most of you already know," he said, "the company has been going through a difficult time recently." A few people around the table nodded slightly, solemnly. I didn't nod slightly, solemnly or otherwise, because I had no idea that the company had been going through a difficult time. As far as I was concerned the company had been going through a wholly unremarkable time.

The owner paused for dramatic effect.

(Pause)

"A very difficult time," the owner continued. The owner paused again, dramatically, to let the news sink in. Or maybe he paused because he just felt like pausing and he didn't answer to anyone. He looked around at the faces looking back at him. The faces that he didn't have to answer to.

"We have been doing all that we can to try and balance the books, but it would appear that our costs are simply too high." His voice filled the room. "And therefore, we are going to have to make some … adjustments." His timing was impeccable. It was as if he had rehearsed. Or maybe it just came naturally to him.

The owner sighed, as if ever so mildly distressed by what he had to say. "So, unfortunately, and I say this with some reluctance," - but not too much, of course - "we are going to have to make some of you redundant."

The owner looked at everyone's faces as he paused, dramatically, to let this momentous news sink in. He liked to pause, dramatically, to let things sink in. It was his way of letting things sink in.

There was muttering around the table. The news was sinking in. I smiled to myself. 'This is good news,' I thought. 'This could be a chance for me.'

The redundancies would be voluntary at first, the owner told us, never once doubting that this was the right course of action to take. He was the kind of man that probably never doubted himself. Doubt, he probably thought, was for other people. And he was probably right.

He also told us that he and the manager would be speaking to everyone individually over the course of the coming days to discuss their future. That meant they would be speaking to me, and I vowed that, when my turn came, I would offer myself as a sacrifice on the altar of the warehouse industry. I would die so that others might live. I could do that for them. I would offer myself.

I was resolved. It was a sacred vow and not to be taken lightly. I imagined that I was doing a good thing.

When the meeting was finished the manager's daughter hurried over to me and grabbed my arm. She was standing so close that I could feel her breasts pressing against me.

"What are you going to do?" she said. "Are you going to leave?" She seemed to be in a state of intense excitement.

"Yes," I said decisively, a faraway look in my eye, or at least I hoped there was a faraway look in my eye. I wanted there to be a faraway look in my eye, but there probably wasn't. "I am going to leave."

I had vowed to offer myself as a sacrifice on the altar of the warehouse industry and that was exactly what I intended to do, as soon as the opportunity presented itself.

I would sacrifice myself so that others could be saved. It would be some sort of grand and selfless gesture.

My Brother's Second Wedding

I'll probably remember my brother's second wedding for as long as I draw breath.

And I imagine that when I'm lying on my deathbed, dying, it will be my brother's second wedding that I'm thinking about. Just before I die.

Even though there will probably be about a million other things I would rather be thinking about just before I die, I will probably be thinking about my brother's second wedding.

That's just the way it goes. You don't get to choose what you remember for as long as you draw breath, or what you think about before you die. You have no choice at all.

I arrived at the church wearing a shabby creased suit that I had stolen from a charity shop. I had stolen the suit because I couldn't afford to buy one, even from a charity shop. I had very little money to survive on in those days; I had just about enough to survive but not enough to buy a suit. Not even from a charity shop.

And so I stole the suit; I didn't really have a choice.

It was not one of my proudest moments. From the moment I entered the shop, the old woman who staffed it eyed me with suspicion. She was leaning against the counter, as if without its support she would simply collapse, and eyeing me with suspicion. She knew that I was up to no good. Don't ask me how, she just knew.

I was very rarely, if truth be told, up to any good.

Her eyes followed me everywhere as I perused the shop's wares looking for a suit that might fit me that I could steal and wear to my brother's wedding.

She knew that whatever I was up to it was no good, and that made me feel more wretched than I already felt, which was pretty wretched. If there was one thing I didn't need it was an old frail woman eyeing me suspiciously to make me feel wretched. I did a good enough job of feeling wretched all by myself without needing an old frail woman to eye me suspiciously.

I found a suit I thought would be appropriate, and took advantage of a moment when the old frail woman was distracted serving another customer to shove it into an empty plastic bag I was carrying.

She knew that whatever I was up to it was no good, but was probably just too old and frail to do anything about it. I walked guiltily out of the shop, carrying the shabby suit in a plastic bag like it was a murder weapon, or a severed head, or something else that I didn't want anyone to notice.

And so, days later, I arrived at the church wearing the shabby suit I had stolen from the charity shop. One thing had led to another.

I examined my appearance in a shop window on my way to the church. The suit I had stolen didn't make me look too great. It was creased and stained in one or two places, and didn't quite fit me properly. My hair was overgrown and hopelessly matted in patches, and I wore a large beard, heavily flecked with white or grey, which I had made no effort to groom. It desperately needed some attention; I desperately needed some attention.

I wondered what people would think. I looked like I was on the run.

'Oh well, no turning back now,' I thought.

A part of me desperately wanted to turn back. But for some reason, the rest of me was determined to see it through. I had come this far. And this far, for me, was pretty far.

The church was crowded. It was full of people who didn't look like they were on the run, and who hadn't stolen their suits from charity shops. It was full of people who bought suits that were the right size for them from proper shops, and then gave them to charity shops when the fashion changed, or when their wardrobe became overpopulated. It was full of people who had conversations with other people all of the time, and thought nothing of it. It was full of people who laughed and smiled, and who always knew what to say and do. And who didn't look like they were on the run. And who weren't trying to not draw attention to themselves.

I was one of the last, if not the last, to arrive. My brother stood expectantly at the front of the church. He looked exactly as you would expect a man who was about to get married to look, and he had aged exactly as I might have imagined him to age, if I had ever imagined how he might have aged, which I hadn't.

He didn't notice me arrive. I kept my eyes on him the whole time; he definitely didn't notice me arrive.

He was talking to someone, standing to his right who I recognised instantly. It was The Undertaker. I had not seen him for about twenty years or so; I had not seen him since the stag trip.

The years had not been kind. He looked bloated. His features were less distinct, less defined; his eyes had sunken beneath the bloating flesh and his nose had reddened and widened. He smiled a bloated watery smile.

My brother and his bride seemed to know an awful lot of people. The church was packed. They seemed to know so many people that it made my head spin.

There were no pews that were entirely empty, so I had to sit next to someone. I sat next to a woman near the back, but reluctantly, because it is hard to not draw attention to yourself when you sit next to someone. People tend to notice when someone sits next to them, especially if that person is wearing a stolen suit that doesn't quite fit them properly, and looks like they are on the run.

The woman who I sat next to was there with her family, which consisted of a man and two children, one male, one female. There was a cosmetic aura surrounding her, which was intoxicating and repelling at the same time. She was dressed exactly like what you would imagine if you were to close your eyes and think of a wedding guest.

The man and the two children were similarly attired. Their outfits had clearly been coordinated. They looked like extras in a movie that required lots of extras dressed exactly as you would expect wedding guests to be dressed.

They were talking excitedly to each other and looked happy, but I couldn't hear a single word they said and I had no idea why they were happy. They were background words and it was background happiness. I wasn't supposed to hear what they were saying and I wasn't supposed to know why they were happy.

The woman looked askance at me, and then shifted herself along the pew a little, away from me, closer to the rest of her family. She looked around to see if anyone else had noticed me, but it didn't appear that anyone had. 'Oh well,' she seemed to shrug, and got on with whatever she was getting on with.

I sat waiting for something to happen, looking straight ahead. I could feel the woman's son looking at me but I stayed looking straight ahead.

There was the sound of shuffling behind me. The din of chatter that had filled the church died away like something else that dies away quite quickly and suddenly with an air of expectation.

"Shhhhhhhhhh-sssssss-ch-ch-aahhh-psssss-ah-ah-sh-sh-haha-shhhhhh," said the crowded church.

Everyone turned around towards the back of the church. Everyone apart from me; I stayed looking straight ahead. I'm the kind of person who, if everyone else turns around, will just keep looking straight ahead. I'm not sure why. I'm just that kind of person.

My brother turned around like everyone else, smiling complacently. He looked older but otherwise exactly as I remembered him. I could tell that, aside from growing older, he hadn't changed one bit.

The church filled with an expectant hush as was customary on such occasions. Everyone in the church was looking at the bride and her entourage, smiling benignly in the way that it is customary to smile on such occasions.

They were smiles that said 'Ah, doesn't she look lovely,' and 'Oh, isn't life sweet after all.'

I stayed looking straight ahead, my gaze fixed on whatever lay straight ahead.

The bride started walking up the aisle to the sound of walking up the aisle music, because it was time for her to start walking up the aisle to the sound of walking up the aisle music. You know how it works.

Every single eye in the church followed the bride as she walked up the aisle apart from mine. I stayed looking straight ahead, but I knew exactly what was happening: my brother was getting married again.

A few rows ahead, I noticed another familiar face: the drooping face of the man I had once known as Ratty. He hadn't just bloated; he had ballooned. He was enormous, and drooped everywhere it is possible for a man to droop. Not without difficulty, he had had to shift his entire body in order to turn his neck enough to be able to see what was going on. I could almost hear his heavy breathing as his eyes followed the bride walking up the aisle.

The wedding progressed as expected. Nothing happened that anyone wasn't expecting to happen. By the end of the ceremony my brother and his bride were married, because that's how these things work.

Everyone looked happy for them and stood as they walked back down the aisle to the sound of walking back down the aisle music, as they were expected to, as you would imagine them to.

I stood as well so as not to draw attention to myself. If there was one thing I knew, and there was, it was how not to draw attention to myself. Nonetheless, I'm sure my brother noticed me as he walked past, and I'm sure that for a brief, almost imperceptible moment a look of disgust and contempt flashed across his features like dark lightning.

The wedding was over, but worse was to come. There is always worse to come.

I looked straight ahead at whatever lay straight ahead.

The Manager's Daughter Exposes Her Left Breast

The redundancy interviews started the next day.
I eagerly awaited the opportunity to carry out my vow: to sacrifice myself on the altar of the warehouse industry.

I imagined that people would think my sacrifice a marvellous and selfless thing.

I was a little put out, then, to discover that there seemed to be a queue of people in front of me who also wished to sacrifice themselves on the altar of the warehouse industry, and who didn't even regard it as a sacrifice of any sort. For some reason I had imagined that everyone else who worked for the company wanted to continue working for the company, but I was wrong. As it turned out I had entirely misjudged the situation.

The guy who carried out odd jobs – the odd-jobs man – was the first to go. The odd-jobs man hobbled everywhere he went and was generally ill-suited to labour of any kind. I don't think I'd ever seen him working, unless you can call smoking roll-ups and talking to anyone who'd listen working, but I don't think you can.

Nevertheless, he'd worked there for years and some people found the idea of him not being employed by the company any longer quite hard to accept. One or two people had to wipe tears from their eyes when he told them that he was leaving, and I thought the fact that one or two people had to wipe tears from their eyes when he told them that he was leaving spoke eloquently in his favour. Even though he served no practical purpose, he would be missed. And really, that's all anyone can ask for. To be missed. You can't ask for much more than that.

After he had spent at least a couple of hours saying his goodbyes in a typically ponderous fashion, I heard him hobble slowly down the exterior metallic skeletal staircase that led from the office to the outside world, taking one step at a time. When he got to the bottom he looked around and saw me standing in the doorway of the warehouse.

"Bye lad," he shouted cheerily in my direction, raising his hand in farewell. We had barely spoken before but he was the kind of guy who would speak to a total stranger as if they were an intimate friend, which is a trait I quite admire to tell the truth.

I didn't respond. I am not at all like the odd-jobs man. Even when I have known people for quite a long time, I speak to them as if they were total strangers.

The next to go was one of the office people, who worked in the office doing office things and who I had never spoken to, but only seen, sometimes, on the other side of a room.

I found this out from the manager's daughter later that same day.

The manager's daughter told me that she could stomach the departure of the odd-jobs man, but what she couldn't stomach was the departure of the office person. And she kept saying the word 'stomach' and it was like she had eaten the odd-jobs man and the office person, and now she was suffering from indigestion.

The office person, she said, was the only person who she could talk to in the whole fucking place.

"I mean she's the only person I can talk to in this whole fucking place!" she told me in a highly agitated state, as if this explained everything.

She was standing in the warehouse, leaning on the counter wearing a loose-fitting blouse. I could see no evidence of a bra. Her eyes sparkled; she was all worked up.

It was a fine spring afternoon.

She had come down to the warehouse, because she needed someone to talk to, and now that the office person had gone, apparently I was her best option. I almost felt a little bit sorry for her; she seemed pretty upset.

"I've known her for years," she said. She was smoking a cigarette as if her life depended on it. "It was me that got her the job here in the first place. Fucking ungrateful! As if, suddenly, working here," – noisy inhalation – "isn't good enough for her. I mean, who else can I talk to up there? It's just fucking selfish, that's what it is. Selfish. She practically begged me to get her a job here. And this is how she repays me!" As she spoke, smoke trickled from her nose and mouth, as if she was on fire. "I tell you what," she said, crushing her butt underfoot, "it's over. Me and her, it's over."

She was pretty upset, but I got the impression that she enjoyed having something to feel angry about, and it suited her. Anger suited her; she wore it well.

Finally, she paused.

"Of course, I'm staying," she said, after a pause. "Someone's got to! There'll be no one left at this rate." She had a talent for overstatement. It came naturally to her.

'Everyone's a martyr to their own cause,' I thought. 'Everyone: me, the manager's daughter, the office person, the odd-jobs man. Everyone.'

We all sacrifice ourselves for ourselves.

There was another pause. It was strangely quiet, as if everyone in the world had paused at exactly the same moment.

We looked as far into the distance as we possibly could, which wasn't too far.

For a moment, it was as if the world had paused.

Nothing happened. Absolutely nothing.

For a moment.

The silence was broken by the sound of boots on the exterior metallic skeletal staircase that led from the outside world to the office. It was a sound that had become very familiar to me. It was the manager. I could tell by his heavy hurried tread, which I had learned to recognise. The manager's daughter turned to me looking suddenly desperate and lost.

"You're not really going to leave, are you?" she said. "You can't leave," she said, continuing as the sound of her father's heavy tread got louder and louder. "I'll have no one to talk to. You can't leave. I won't let you leave."

I wondered why she seemed to care so much, because I couldn't understand why she seemed to care so much. I had certainly never given her a reason to care so much, or at all to tell the truth.

The sound of the manager's heavy tread got louder as he approached, which was inevitable. Things inevitably get louder as they approach.

"Don't leave. Please!" said the manager's daughter, desperately. I wondered why she seemed so desperate; it almost made me feel a little sorry for her.

Before I could reply, the manager appeared in the doorway of the warehouse. He was dressed up in a pale blue shirt that was tucked neatly into crisp beige trousers. He only ever dressed up when the owner was around, trying to make a good impression, and he looked uncomfortable. All day long it looked as though he was having an argument with his clothes, and I'm not sure if the owner was too impressed anyway.

He looked at his daughter and me with distaste, as if seeing us together had a horrible sour taste. And I can imagine it did. I imagine it would taste pretty horrible to see your daughter talking to someone like me.

"What the fuck are you doing here?" the manager asked his daughter, as if it was beyond his powers of comprehension to understand what she could possibly be doing in the warehouse talking to someone like me.

There were large sweat patches under each of his arms. He was the kind of person who always had large sweat patches under each of his arms on a warm day. It was quite unsightly to tell the truth.

His daughter didn't reply.

"Well?" he said, because his daughter hadn't replied.

"Mind your own bloody business," said the manager's daughter. They didn't seem to have a great relationship. They were never pleasant with other. You would never have imagined that there were any feelings of affection between them.

The manager seethed inwardly. He had no idea how to handle his daughter. He had no idea how to handle anyone. He certainly wasn't a people person. The dark patches under his arms expanded their empire.

"Come upstairs," he said to her. "We need to talk."

He looked at me as if he had just tasted dog shit for the first time, and was surprised to discover that it tasted even worse than he had anticipated.

"And you." He meant me. I was 'you' to him. "Get back to work while you've still got a fucking job."

He turned around and walked out, towards the exterior metallic skeletal staircase that led from the outside world to the office above. The manager's daughter flashed me a knowing look. She might have rolled her eyes or something like that. I can't really remember. But let's just say she rolled her eyes. It doesn't matter if she really did or not.

The manager's daughter rolled her eyes and trudged out of the warehouse, and as she did so she seemed to have an idea. She stopped in her tracks, as if she had just had an idea.

She glanced ahead in the direction of her father to check if he could see her, and then, turning back to me, lifted her loose-fitting blouse and exposed her left breast, which bounced briefly in the sunlight before she let her blouse fall. She giggled and disappeared, following in her father's wake.

I stood there open-mouthed. I remember feeling a sense of wonder that manager's daughters could have such treasures constantly at their disposal, such treasures as left breasts. I really thought it was amazing.

I stood in the doorway of the warehouse. There was nothing more pressing to do, so I closed my eyes against the sunlight of a fine spring afternoon.

I thought about the manager's daughter's left breast; I tried to picture the manager's daughter's left breast in my mind, which, for some reason, was not as easy as it sounds. Somehow, I couldn't get it quite right.

For a moment I considered reneging on my vow to sacrifice myself on the altar of the warehouse industry, so as to stay as close as possible to the manager's daughter's left breast. But then I decided that I couldn't allow myself to be distracted so easily from my avowed purpose. I had to remain firm. I had made a vow after all.

For a moment, it was unnaturally quiet, as if everyone in the world had, by entire coincidence or prior arrangement, paused at exactly the same moment.

My eyes were closed against the sunlight. I tried hard to picture the manager's daughter's left breast in my mind, but already the memory of it was fading.

The Nearest Town

We continued drifting downriver. Or upriver, depending on your perspective. A moody silence had descended upon the men I was with. A calm before the storm sort of silence. A silence that was full of what the night might hold.

After my sojourn on the small island I was full of an inexpressible rage, which I could find no way of expressing and which soured everything, which was already pretty sour to begin with.

We drifted past trees and fields that were slowly dissolving into the encroaching darkness, until we came within sight of the nearest town.

The nearest town crouched nervously in the uncertain light of dusk, as if it somehow knew that it would be better for everyone, including itself, if we didn't notice that it was the nearest town.

But, even in the half-light of dusk, a nearest town cannot help but be noticed, even when it's trying not to be.

It looked like one of those towns that exist solely out of habit and have nothing left to say to the world.

My brother and his friends disappeared inside the boat to get ready, which meant putting on clean shirts and shiny leather shoes. I didn't have a clean shirt or shiny leather shoes so I stayed outside, quietly wishing that some catastrophe would quickly end my life and the lives of everyone I had ever met or would ever meet.

At last they were ready to go. They assembled on the deck of the boat in high spirits; their laughter echoed in the stillness of the hour.

I remained apart, pretending that I was quite happy where I was.

My brother said something and they all jumped ashore. They began walking along the towpath towards the lights of the nearest town, which hid behind trees hoping that no one would notice. But we had noticed.

My brother led the way purposefully, as if he knew exactly what he was doing. The rest of his friends followed, as if they knew exactly what was expected of them. I followed too, not really feeling like I had much of a choice.

I trailed a few feet behind the rest of the group, and was largely ignored by them. I say 'largely' ignored because at one point The Undertaker told me to 'keep up' in an affable manner.

"Come on mate," he said affably. "Keep up." But that was all he said.

"OK," I said, but I don't think he heard me; he had already turned his attention elsewhere.

I was having a miserable time, but I'm sure the fault was all my own. I'm sure I had nobody to blame but myself. No one else seemed to be having a miserable time. Everyone else seemed to be enjoying themselves perfectly well.

As I trailed a few feet behind the rest of the group a resolution formed in my mind: I would try not to have a miserable time; I would try to be sociable; I would try to get on with the men I was with. That was the resolution that, for some reason, formed in my mind. I guess I decided that I had to do something. The way things were was almost unbearable.

For a moment my newfound resolve almost made me feel quite happy; I almost bounced along thinking of things I might say. I might even have whistled, but I've never been able to whistle, so it seems unlikely.

It didn't take us long to get to the nearest pub; the nearest pub is never too far away. That's the whole idea behind nearest pubs: the whole idea behind nearest pubs is that they're never too far away.

The Undertaker was buying drinks for my brother and one or two of the other men, who live on in my mind only as blurry indistinct smudges of man-shaped colour. I stood next to him.

"Do you want a drink, mate?" he said.

He was offering to buy me a drink! I felt pathetically grateful. It was a strangely pleasant feeling. I wondered if everything was going to be OK after all.

"Oh, thanks," I said, sounding more pathetic than I wanted to.

"What would you like?" said The Undertaker affably. He had an affable way about him, there's no denying it.

"Could I get a pint, please?" The way I said it, it sounded like a question, even though there was no need for it to.

"A pint of what?" he said, with more than a hint of light mockery in his tone.

I didn't really know. I was still young enough not to really know what I wanted a pint of.

"Beer?" I said hopefully, sounding pitifully unsure of myself.

The Undertaker laughed indulgently, but thankfully didn't ask any more questions. He bought me a pint of some sort of beer and all things considered, I thought the night had started reasonably well. It had certainly started as well as could reasonably be expected.

My brother and his friends squeezed around a table. It really was quite a squeeze and, as the last to arrive, there was no room for me to sit down. No more squeezing was possible.

I looked around the bar as panic started to rise within me. I felt almost unbearably self-conscious, even though no one was paying any attention to me whatsoever. I couldn't just stand there. That would be awful, unthinkable. And besides, I was determined to be sociable, to be a part of the group.

I spotted a chair on the other side of the room. Not without difficulty, I went and fetched it. I'm the kind of person who can't even do very simple things, like fetching a chair, without difficulty.

I placed the chair next to the table that my brother and his friends were squeezed around. I sat down awkwardly, trying to fit myself into as small a space as possible. There was a moment of awkward silence, but it was only a moment and I couldn't really tell if anyone else found it particularly awkward, or even noticed it at all. It was hard to tell.

"Here's to a messy fucking night," said Ratty loudly holding his glass aloft, seemingly unaware that there had been a moment of awkward silence. "Cheers motherfuckers," he continued. Glasses clinked. Cheers.

"Cheers," said all the men I was with. The motherfuckers.

I raised my glass awkwardly, trying to join in, but I was outside of the circle of intimacy. The Undertaker seemed to notice my awkwardness and sympathetically clinked glasses with me once he was done with everyone else.

"Cheers, mate," he said.

"Cheers," I mumbled.

Cheers.

They started talking about women. Or sex I should say. They were talking about sex.

"So," Ratty said boorishly, addressing my brother, "you managed to get it up last night! I'm sure your bride will be delighted!" He laughed.

A couple of the blurry indistinct smudges of man-shaped colour sniggered uncertainly. They weren't really sure if it was all right to laugh at this. You could never really be sure if my brother was going to be able to take a joke or not. He was the kind of person who only had a sense of humour when he felt like having one. He was the kind of person it was sometimes hard to read.

The Undertaker sat gravely, like a tombstone, sipping his beer.

"Oh, fuck off," said my brother. He didn't seem particularly amused on this occasion. "At least I'm getting some," he added, looking quite pleased with himself. It didn't take much for my brother to look quite pleased with himself.

Ratty, however, was not one to back down from an implied challenge. The implication that he had a lacklustre sex life could simply not go unchallenged.

"Oh, don't worry about me," he said, "I'm getting plenty. And I don't have to pay for it either!" Ratty laughed, but this time no one else joined him. Implying that my brother had to pay for sex was a step too far; it was crossing a line that few dared cross.

The Undertaker sat gravely watching a familiar scenario play out as if it was of absolutely no interest to him at all. He wore an inscrutable expression that fitted him snugly.

My brother looked a little uncomfortable. I don't think he was entirely comfortable with sex talk. He was quite prim really. But Ratty wasn't; undaunted, he continued.

"Fucked a girl last week," he continued. "She was fucking wasted!"

"She must have been!" someone said, and people laughed. It was always OK to have a laugh at Ratty's expense. He had built his entire character on being able to take a joke.

"She was!" said Ratty, proudly. He didn't seem to mind the laughter at his expense. Or at least he acted as if he didn't seem to mind. He had built his entire character on never really seeming to mind about anything, or at least acting as if he never really seemed to mind about anything.

You can never really be too sure if people are really doing something, or just acting as if they are really doing something.

"She was virtually unconscious by the time I got her upstairs to bed. She let me do anything to her!"

He laughed coarsely like the loathsome and unlikeable character he was. Most of the other men were laughing too. Ratty, despite being loathsome and unlikeable, had quite an infectious laugh, and people seemed to like him.

"Sounds like you were fucking a corpse," said my brother, without a hint of humour.

The Undertaker's ears pricked and he showed a flicker of interest in the conversation.

Ratty took a massive gulp from his glass of beer. There was a moment of silence, but it was hard to tell if anyone found the moment of silence awkward or not.

The Undertaker broke the momentary silence. "So, you raped her then," he said in a deadpan tone.

My brother laughed maniacally, as if this was the funniest thing he had ever heard anyone say.

But Ratty, as usual, was undaunted. He was building an extension to his character by being undaunted by whatever came his way.

"Best sex I ever had," he said, and laughed coarsely, as if being called a rapist was the funniest thing in the world.

Everyone round the table was laughing now, even The Undertaker whose laughter was sedate and floated to the ground like the ashes of a loved one.

I tried to laugh but it just wouldn't come. My mouth obstinately refused to frame itself to laugh. All I could manage was a weak, unsteady smile, which no one took the least notice of anyway.

Now others around the table began telling stories of their own real or imagined sexual conquests. The Undertaker became animated.

"I'll tell you what," he said gravely, as if speaking to everyone at once, but also to no one in particular. "It's the undertaking business you want to be in if it's transgressive sex you're after. All those grieving widows, daughters, sisters, nieces, cousins, mistresses. They're literally begging for it half the time. Fucked a girl recently while her mother's ashes were still smouldering. Practically begged me."

He smiled arcanely as if he was the only person in the world who knew how great it was to fuck a grieving daughter while her mother's ashes were still smouldering.

He looked around satisfied. Everyone took a sip of their drink at the same time, apart from me.

This was my chance to join in with an anecdote of my own. 'After all,' I thought, 'if you want to be sociable you have to join in with an anecdote of your own.'

But I didn't. I searched through my stock of anecdotes, but I didn't find anything I felt was appropriate. I didn't exactly have a wide stock of anecdotes. The shelves were pretty bare. I could have told them about the time I tried to have sex behind a skip in a car park with the girl I used to live with when I worked at the pie factory, but I didn't. I decided not to. It wasn't a great story anyway.

Instead, I was silent and said nothing. Nothing at all. Not even one word.

Long-Lost Brother

It was my brother's second wedding.
I should never have gone. The arguments had been stacked pretty heavily in favour of not going. But I still went, harbouring some forlorn, indistinct hope.

And as I shuffled into the old country house where the reception was to be held, with the other wedding guests, I wished that I had declined the invitation. I wished that I had returned the invitation to sender with the words, 'Not known at this address', scrawled on the envelope. That would have been so easy.

I felt like I was on the run, and I felt like I was going to be captured at any moment.

The line of people waiting to enter the house moved slowly. Before they could enter the old country house, the wedding guests had to shake hands with my brother and kiss his bride on both cheeks, as was customary on such occasions, and this took time. But most people were chatting amicably with someone or other as they waited and didn't seem to mind.

I was already wondering how much more of this I could take. I guess I'm the kind of person who spends a lot of time wondering how much more they can take.

There were a lot of guests. My brother would have insisted that there were a lot of guests. Lots of guests sends a message to the world. The guests looked just like you would imagine a lot of wedding guests to look like if you were to close your eyes and imagine a lot of wedding guests.

The guests shuffled forward. I seemed to be the only person who had no one to talk to. Not that I would have known what to do if I did have.

Inevitably, my turn came, as I knew it inevitably must. And I think somehow, for some reason, I wanted my turn to come. A forlorn threadbare hope still pursued me.

My brother looked at me stonily, for the first time in countless years, giving absolutely nothing away. His face was covered in lines I had never seen before. I hadn't noticed them earlier; you could only really see them when you were close up.

"Thanks for coming," he said quietly as he shook my hand, as if there was absolutely nothing unusual about the two of us standing face-to-face and shaking hands. A sudden memory of childhood flickered in my mind. It wasn't a memory of an event, but a memory of a feeling. It was a memory of admiring him, of looking up to him. But I was a different person then. I was a child who couldn't be blamed for anything.

"Glad you could make it," he said, as if he really was glad I had made it, which seemed unlikely.

He looked me up and down and grimaced, before quickly shifting his attention to the next person in the line, as if he couldn't bear to look at me for even a moment longer.

"Great to see you," I heard him say to the next person in the line. "So glad you could make it." He greeted them warmly, whoever they were, as if they were his long-lost brother who he hadn't seen for countless years.

"Congratulations," I managed to mumble at his bride, who was standing next to him.

"Um ... thanks," she said doubtfully, as if she suspected that I wasn't really supposed to be there.

I tried, but couldn't bring myself to make eye contact. I'm not sure how hard I tried; it can't be that difficult to make eye contact with someone, can it? Maybe I didn't try hard enough.

"Who was that?" I heard her ask my brother as I walked away. She had a sweet voice. It was the kind of voice that, for some reason, made me want to close my eyes.

"I'll tell you later," I heard my brother reply.

I considered leaving, running away, being somewhere else, never coming back.

I wondered how much more I could take.

Little Girl

The wedding guests were taking their seats. They seemed to know where to sit. I wondered how. Then I saw the seating plan, as if that explained everything.

I scanned the seating plan, hoping that I wouldn't see my name, hoping that it had all been a big mistake and that I could go home.

But no, there it was: my name.

Seeing my name on the seating plan made me want to cry. It cost me a great effort not to just burst out in tears right there in front of the seating plan.

My name and I had grown apart. We hadn't spoken for years. It was almost as if it had a life of its own, and had nothing to do with me whatsoever. It might once have had something to do with me, but now it had nothing to do with me whatsoever.

But it was still my name, whether or not it had anything to do with me whatsoever. I went and sat down in my seat, in accordance with the seating plan.

There was no one else sitting at the table that I had been allocated to apart from a little girl. The other wedding guests, who were supposed to be sitting at the table, were most probably mingling at the bar, drink in hand, exactly as you would expect wedding guests to be mingling if they had a few minutes to spare before the meal was due to start.

There was a little folded piece of card on the table with my name on it. I felt tears welling but I fought them back.

I had been positioned next to the little girl.

She was a pert little girl and sat impossibly upright in her chair, searching the room as if looking for something to do, or someone she could do something with. I guessed she was about ten or eleven, but I had no frame of reference. I didn't have much to do with children, as you can probably imagine.

The little girl looked at me searchingly, as I sat down, in that odd unabashed way that some kids look at strange old men.

"Hello," she said as I sat down, without a second thought. I sat down and stared straight ahead solemnly. I tried to ignore her.

She looked at me searchingly. I could tell that she wasn't going to let me ignore her.

"Are you all right?" she said.

"Yes, I'm fine," I said, convincing no one, not even the little girl.

I was lying, of course, but it felt OK to lie to a child. Lying to children is a thing people do. Hardly anything people say to children is true.

She didn't look convinced. "Are you sure?" she asked.

"I'm sure," I said, irritably.

"Well, you don't look fine," she said.

And she was right, of course. I was a mess. I wasn't fine. There were lots of things wrong. It was almost overwhelming how many things were wrong.

I wondered how much more I could take. I considered leaving. I considered saying, 'Excuse me,' and walking briskly out of the room. And I imagined breaking into a hurried jog as soon as I was out of the old country house and breathing fresh air again. And I thought about what a great relief it would be to breathe fresh air again. Fresh air's amazing. Never take fresh air for granted.

There was no fresh air inside the house; it had all been used hundreds of times before. There was nothing fresh about it whatsoever.

I considered leaving, but for some reason, I didn't. Instead, I just wondered how much more I could take.

"Who are you?" the little girl asked, as if it was a perfectly reasonable question to ask. And then, when I didn't respond immediately: "Do you know mother and father?"

"I'm the groom's brother," I replied eventually. There was no avoiding her questions. The little girl looked a little confused.

"But then, why aren't you sitting on the groom's table?" Little girls have a habit of getting to the heart of the matter without wasting too much time. "Why weren't you the best man?" Questions piled on top on questions like dust on an old picture.

"Well, my brother and I don't get along," I said. "To tell the truth we don't like each other much. We haven't spoken for years." Uncharacteristically, I decided on a course of openness and honesty. Maybe I thought the little girl would understand.

"How many years?" asked the little girl, as if this was of some vital importance.

"I don't know. Quite a few. Many." I sighed.

"Then why are you here at all?" She was trying to work it all out, but she had no frame of reference. I guess she didn't have too much to do with strange old men. I guess that she had only ever met people who got on fine with their brothers.

"That's a good question," I said knowingly, thinking about the conversation I had had with the invitation, as if it was all the invitation's fault.

"Well, what's the answer?" She was that kind of kid: everything she said was a question, and every question had to have an answer. She wasn't yet ready to accept that some questions don't have answers.

The little girl looked at me as if I made no sense at all.

Other people were now hovering around the table about to take their seats. I looked around at the faces hovering above me. They looked exactly as you would expect the faces hovering above me to look.

I was saved from having to answer further questions by the appearance of the little girl's mother.

"Hi darling," said the little girl's mother. She looked almost exactly like I might have imagined her to look, if I had imagined how she might look, which I hadn't. She looked like a bigger, older, more motherly version of the little girl.

The little girl's mother glanced at me, and then back at her daughter. "You've made another friend, I see," she said cheerily, showing no sign of concern that her daughter had 'made friends' with a strange old man with a scraggly beard and unkempt hair, who looked like he was on the run. She didn't seem too concerned at all, which I thought was strange.

The little girl rolled her eyes, affecting exasperation, as if her mother was the most annoying person in the world.

Her mother extended her hand for me to shake, which I did unconvincingly, and told me her name, which I immediately forgot.

"Hello," I mumbled. "Nice to meet you," I said, as if I too were a little kid, even though I was far from a little kid. I didn't tell her my name; I couldn't bring myself to utter it aloud.

"He's the groom's brother," said the little girl proudly, as if she had uncovered a great secret.

"Oh," said her mother. She looked at me with a mixture of fascination and disgust, as if she had heard things about me and could now, finally, put a face to the things she had heard about me.

Other people were taking their seats and, thankfully, the little girl's mother's attention was distracted.

The little girl was also distracted. She had other things to occupy her rampant curiosity. She studied the other people who were now taking their seats with that searching little girl look of hers. She was getting her questions ready, no doubt.

One or two people that she knew, or that knew her, might have noticed her and said something like, 'Hi honey,' or, 'Hello sweetheart,' or, 'My, haven't you grown,' or some other such thing that people say when they see a child that they know.

And she might have replied in a pert voice, 'Hello Uncle John,' or, 'Hi, Auntie Joan.' It was always uncle or auntie something with her. I was probably uncle something with her: 'uncle strange old man,' or 'uncle groom's brother,' or something like that.

"Hi gorgeous," said a familiar voice. I looked up.

It was Ratty. Not without difficulty, Ratty was taking his seat.

Hello uncle Ratty.

Ratty Sits Down

Ratty sat down. The edges of the room started to bleed into its centre, if that makes any sense. I felt dizzy. I thought I might pass out and fall off my seat.

Forces were at work that I couldn't control.

Ratty had grown so large that he was only able to sit down with the assistance of a thin pale woman. Even then, he was not able to sit down without great difficulty. It didn't seem like there was much Ratty could do anymore without great difficulty. He was wheezing and panting; drops of sweat were trudging their way down his forehead. The thin pale woman looked fed up, like she was fed up with helping Ratty to sit down or stand up or whatever else she may have helped him do.

He was a gigantic man. As I watched him sit down I imagined what he would look like naked. I'm not sure why. It was just what I imagined. I didn't particularly want to imagine what he would look like naked, but I had no choice. It just happened.

Once Ratty was safely seated, the thin pale woman took her seat next to him. She looked slightly younger than the invalid that she looked after, though she could easily have been slightly older than him. It was hard to tell. There was something ageless about her. Like she had always been.

She was wearing a simple black dress, which contrasted with her pale skin and made her look almost like a spectre, or a shadow, or something like that. There was a quiet gravity about her that formed a marked contrast with her fleshy companion.

She looked almost familiar, and I wondered if I had seen her somewhere before.

More people arrived at the table and, having sought out their names, took their seats, as they were expected to.

A gaunt ashen-faced man took the other seat next to Ratty's, and the two men, who evidently knew each other from somewhere or other, greeted each other warmly. The gaunt ashen-faced man smirked as he made what I judged by his expression to be a particularly droll comment, and Ratty shook with laughter. The laughter had a disagreeable effect and he started coughing and spluttering; he was almost choking. It was as if he was literally dying of laughter.

The gaunt man recoiled and the thin pale woman started patting his back distractedly, as if she had performed a similar action about a million times before, and was not at all concerned, but was rather, if she felt anything, a little fed up.

Eventually the coughing spluttered to a halt. It had got to the point where the coughing either spluttered to a halt or he dropped dead. But he didn't drop dead; instead the coughing spluttered to a halt, and the man I knew as Ratty slowly recovered his composure.

A large part of me wished he had dropped dead, but it made no difference at all what a large part of me wished. Despite a large part of me wishing he had dropped dead, Ratty slowly recovered his composure.

Oriental Crackers of Some Description

I'd better carry on with this story.
First somebody said, "I'm fucking starving," which was the cue to leave.

"I'm fucking starving," said one of the men I was with.

"Yeah, me too," said another.

"Right, let's go," said a third.

And then they finished their drinks and left the pub behind.

That is how it works. There is machinery behind everything. There are no accidents. Things don't just happen. A group of men don't just finish their drinks and leave the pub behind just like that. Someone has to say 'I'm fucking starving' – or something like that – first because that is how it works.

Anyway: on with the story.

I lagged behind the rest of the group as I had decided to return the chair I had been sitting on to where I had found it. I had started to leave with the rest of the group, but then I looked back and saw the chair and, for some reason, felt that I ought to return the chair to where I found it. I think I thought the chair looked lonely or something, as if chairs are even remotely concerned about things like being lonely. Maybe I felt that if I didn't return the chair to where I found it, the chair would feel out of sorts and its day would be ruined, as if chairs even notice whether their day has been ruined or not.

I actually felt sorry for the chair. It had been good to me. We had an understanding.

"There you go," I said, when the chair was back where it belonged.

"Thanks," said the chair. "Much appreciated."

"You're welcome," I said. "Enjoy the rest of your evening."

"And you," said the chair.

"I'll try," I said. "See you later."

"See ya," said the chair.

Anyway: on with the story. The story must go on. Until it's finished. Because that is how stories work: they go on and on and on until they are finished. They don't just get stuck on a talking chair and stop somewhere near the middle. They go on and on and on until they are finished.

The group of men I was with raucously wound its way through the churchyards, the cobbled streets and the market square of the nearest town looking for somewhere to satisfy the appetites of its members. I lagged behind. Despite my resolution to be sociable, I wasn't having much success. I had more or less given up to tell the truth, and found it a relief to be lagging behind the group of men I was with.

After a while, the group of men stopped outside a restaurant that served oriental food of some description. They began to inspect the menu, loudly jostling each other and sharing jokes, as if inspecting the menu of a restaurant was the most fun a group of men could possibly have.

Maybe it was. Who am I to judge?

They stood outside the restaurant for several minutes jostling and joking, and looking at the menu, as if it was one of those pictures that if you stare at for ages turns into something else, like a pirate ship, or a candlelit room, or something like that.

Eventually, someone said, "Come on, let's just go in. I'm fucking starving," which was the cue for the group of men to enter the restaurant.

There is machinery behind everything. Don't even question it.

The group of men filed into the restaurant one by one. I followed because I didn't really have a choice. What else could I have done?

Most people never really have a choice. You just do what you've got to do.

I found myself inside the restaurant. I looked around bewildered, as if I had never seen a restaurant before.

The waiter showed the men I was with to their table. Ratty thanked the waiter, imitating his accent, which was different to his own. One or two of the men I was with sniggered, as if laughing at the way someone spoke was their absolute favourite thing to do in the world. The waiter, who didn't look best pleased, showed us to our table.

The men I was with perused the menu exactly as you would expect a group of men to peruse a menu. They didn't take it too seriously, as you can probably imagine. It was all a big joke to the group of men. Everything was a big joke to the group of men.

I didn't have too much money, so when it was time to order, I ordered the cheapest item on the menu, which happened to be a bowl of oriental crackers of some description.

The food ordered, the men I was with set about their business, which was getting drunk and making each other laugh, both of which they were very good at. Getting drunk and making each other laugh came naturally to them. It was like getting drunk and making each other laugh had been invented with them in mind. But, seemingly, they hadn't been invented with me in mind. I was surrounded by the burble of drunken men, and had no idea what to say or do.

I counted my money for something to do. It didn't take long, and only served to confirm what I already knew: that I didn't have much money. But it was, at least, something to do.

When I had finished counting my money, I examined the posters on the wall. I had to do something. The posters depicted idealised views of nature. There were waterfalls and forests, that sort of thing. One or two had vague aspirational slogans like, 'Explore your dreams,' or 'Discover freedom.' But again, examining the posters on the wall didn't take long. There wasn't much to examine, and it would have looked strange if I had examined them for too long.

For a moment I pretended to be particularly interested in something behind me, but that didn't take long either. There's only so long you can pretend to be particularly interesting in something behind you, and it's not too long.

Thankfully, the food arrived promptly. I think they were trying to get rid of us as quickly as possible, which was fair enough. If someone makes fun of the way you speak, trying to get rid of them as quickly as possible is fair enough.

My bowl of oriental crackers of some description was the first thing to arrive, and I was momentarily relieved because it did, at least for a moment, give me something to do. It focused my attention.

But eating the crackers didn't take long. There was nothing to them really. They were mostly air.

For Starters

The wedding guests slowly took their seats. Wedding guests don't rush for anyone. They take their seats slowly, in their own time. There is no possible reason for them to rush.

They took their seats while clasping drinks and lost in conversation with someone or other about their holiday to somewhere or other, or about someone or other who did something or other, or about whatever the hell you would expect wedding guests to be talking about as they take their seats.

To be honest you probably don't need me to spell out every little detail. I'm sure you've been to a wedding before. You know how these things work.

I was getting impatient. I was beginning to think that this wretched day would never end.

I wondered how much more of it I could take. I considered leaving. Leaving was pretty much all I thought about. But I didn't. Instead, for some reason, I stayed exactly where I was, as if I really had no choice but to stay exactly where I was. As if there was some sort of reason why I absolutely had to stay exactly where I was.

Ratty had recovered from his coughing fit, and was chatting amiably with the gaunt ashen-faced man next to him. It was a quick, but not a full, recovery. Ratty, I thought, looked a little pale after his ordeal. The colour, normally so robust, had faded a little from his cheeks.

The little girl next to me was chatting away to her mother, asking all sorts of questions. Her questions were like the coaches of a train clattering over the tracks.

The sounds of chatter came from all directions at once. I felt like I was under siege and a fatal, devastating blow could come from any direction at any time. I was on the brink. It was touch and go, whatever that means.

I had to close my eyes and rock slightly in my chair to try and make some sense of it all.

I realise this makes me sound crazy, but I'm not crazy. I just wasn't used to a huge amount of chatter. I'm sure anyone would have difficulty adjusting to something they're not used to. It doesn't mean they're crazy.

Without any warning at all a hush sucked all the noise out of the room. My brother and his bride were making their grand entrance. They were expected to make a grand entrance, and so they were making a grand entrance. That's just how these things work.

The wedding guests stood to receive the bride and groom. There was loud applause, and a handful of the livelier and more enthusiastic wedding guests whooped and cheered. My brother and his bride smiled and mouthed their thanks as they wound their way past all the other tables to their seats.

The happy couple sat down; everyone else sat down. Somehow, everyone else knew what to do. Everyone seemed to know how these things worked.

I gritted my teeth and focused. 'You can do it,' I told myself, over and over again inside my head. But I wasn't sure what I could do or how I was going to do it. Somehow,

I knew that when the time came, I wouldn't really have a choice. I would just do what I had to do.

Now that everyone was seated, well-dressed waiters began bringing out plate after plate of meticulously arranged food.

Ratty fell silent while he ate. He clearly enjoyed his food too much to continue chatting amiably with the gaunt ashen-faced man, or to respond with more than a shrug to the occasional remarks deposited in his ear by the pale thin woman. Enjoying his food seemed to use up all his concentration.

I had been watching him since he sat down, but up until this point he hadn't noticed me. However, when he had finished his first course, and had wiped his mouth with a napkin and sighed, he sat back and noticed me staring right at him.

For once my stare did not waver. I had expected my stare, once it had been discovered, to scamper to the other side of the room, to hide under a chair or table, to peer out from under the tablecloth. But no, my stare did none of those things; my stare did not waver.

Ratty met my unwavering stare with a stare of his own. It was a quizzical stare. It was the kind of absent stare of a man who knows he recognises someone but is not sure from where or when.

'He ought to recognise me,' I thought. 'At the very least he ought to recognise me.'

In his defence, my face was much altered since he had last seen it. It was a very different face to the one he had known twenty years previously: it was drawn and haggard; it was pinched and gnarled. It had been beaten by time. Nonetheless, he ought to have recognised me. It was the least he could have done. But his stare remained quizzical. He had no idea who I was.

A face that he did know, approaching from behind, distracted him. It was the bloated face of The Undertaker.

"Still fucking enormous," said The Undertaker, and laughed. The gaunt ashen-faced man laughed too.

"Still fucking corpses," said Ratty, giving as good as he got. Over the years Ratty had built his reputation on giving as good as he got.

They spoke to each other as if it was still twenty years ago and nothing else had happened. They seemed to find each other incredibly amusing and each laughed at almost everything the other said, which is what friends are for, I suppose.

The conversation didn't last long. The Undertaker was doing the rounds. At weddings some people do the rounds, as you can probably already know. The Undertaker was one such person.

He patted Ratty on the back and scanned the table as if to see if there was anyone else worth saying hello to. He paid no more attention to me than if I had been an unnecessary piece of furniture that he hadn't noticed, but then his gaze stopped on the little girl sitting next to me. He scampered over towards her.

"Hello darling," he said, bending down to kiss her on the top of her head.

"Hi dad," replied the little girl.

"You enjoying yourself?" asked The Undertaker. Dad.

"Yes, thank you," she replied. She didn't ask him any questions, which seemed odd, given her propensity for asking questions. There seemed to be a distance between them, which I could not account for. It was as if they were miles apart.

The Undertaker exchanged a few businesslike words with the girl's mother and then he was off. Doing the rounds. He seemed to be enjoying himself, and there was no reason at all why he shouldn't have been. He was expected to enjoy himself. It was expected of him.

The first course was done with and the dirtied plates were taken away. The little girl ran off somewhere like kids do. The thing is with kids is that they can't stay still for too long.

I wondered how much more I could take, and thought about leaving. I pictured myself getting up and walking off and tasting fresh air and never having to talk to anyone ever again. I thought about leaving almost continuously. But I didn't leave. I stayed exactly where I was, as if I had planned to stay exactly where I was all along.

I had come this far. The worst was over. Or at least that's what I told myself. That's how I convinced myself not to leave. But the worst wasn't over. The worst had only just begun.

This Far

The food kept coming. Plate after plate of artfully arranged food kept being placed carefully in front of me. I didn't really have a choice. No one asked me if I wanted any of it.

The little girl had returned and ate politely; her manners were impeccable. Opposite her, Ratty ate wolfishly, forming a contrast.

I hardly touched my food. I didn't even know whether I was hungry or not, but I certainly didn't have much of an appetite. I only touched it at all for show; I didn't want to draw attention to myself by not touching my food at all. Not touching your food at all is a thing people might notice.

The truth is I wasn't used to eating fine food; I survived on bread and cheese like a medieval peasant. I usually ate with my hands. In fact, come to think of it, I always used my hands. I had no idea what to do with a plate of artfully arranged food. You definitely weren't supposed to eat it with your hands.

When she had finished her meal, the little girl looked at my plate – still full of food – and then up at me sympathetically, as if she knew exactly how sad and pathetic I really was. She knew exactly what was going on that little girl. I don't know how, but she did.

"Why don't you and your brother get on?" she said, without preamble. Kids don't really do preamble. Preamble is an adult's game. She just asked me why my brother and I didn't get on like it was the most natural thing to do in the world.

"We just don't like each other," I said, because I knew she wouldn't let me ignore her and I couldn't think of anything else to say.

"But why not?" she asked. "There must be a reason."

'Why?' I thought. 'Why does there have to be a reason?' I didn't say anything, I just wondered why there always had to be a reason.

That's the problem with human beings, I realised. The problem with human beings is that there always has to be a reason for everything. Sometimes, there just isn't a reason for something, but human beings find that hard to accept. As far as human beings are concerned there always has to be a reason for everything.

I knew she wouldn't understand. People never understand the things that are really important.

I was beginning to get annoyed. I didn't want to answer any more questions. Just being there used up all my energy; I didn't have any left to answer questions.

I rubbed my eyes, as if that might help. I couldn't respond because there was no answer to her question, or at least, I had no words to articulate an answer. No words and no energy.

The little girl continued to look at me as if I made absolutely no sense at all. Thankfully, the questions stopped. She probably realised that she wasn't going to get any more out of me, and so it wasn't worth trying too hard. After a few minutes she ran off in search of something else to do.

Time passed; it had no choice. The waiters began bringing out the desserts, rushing about with purpose, making the most of every second, as if every second is a thing worth being made the most of.

The desserts were elaborate constructions, and while Ratty ate wolfishly, demolishing the elaborate construction within seconds, the gaunt ashen-faced man next to him ate surgically, as if he were performing a life-saving operation. He seemed to know exactly what he was doing.

I messed my dessert about a bit so that no one would notice me not eating my dessert.

I wondered how much more I could take. I considered leaving, but it didn't make any sense to leave.

I had come this far, which was pretty far.

The Cheapest Whisky

By the time that the men I was with were served the food they had ordered, I had absolutely nothing to do.

I had eaten the oriental crackers of some description that I had ordered, and that were mostly air, and there was absolutely nothing else to do.

I thought about wandering around outside until the men I was with had finished eating, but I didn't wish to attract any unnecessary attention to myself by getting up and leaving the table, so I stayed exactly where I was. We were really getting on quite well, the men I was with and I, pretending that I didn't exist. We had discovered a sort of equilibrium that I did not wish to disturb. Besides, I even doubted my ability to take such decisive action, which is exactly as sad and pathetic as it sounds.

I felt like a ghost who no one believed in, haunting itself.

I sipped the beer I was drinking as slowly as I possibly could, not wanting it to end, honestly believing that it was my only companion in the world and that when it was finished I would be utterly alone. I became quite depressed by the thought of finishing the beer I was drinking. It is absurd to sentimentalise a liquid, but that was what I had been reduced to.

I sat there awkwardly for the rest of the meal with nothing to do. I didn't speak to anyone and no one spoke to me. We were all doing a fine job of pretending that I didn't exist.

The time passed. At some point the meal was deemed to be over. One of the men said, "Right then, shall we?" and stood up, which the other men took as a signal to stand up too. Once they had stood up there was nothing to do but leave.

After the restaurant the group of men I was with headed loudly towards the nearest pub, like a ship in a storm.

I followed at a distance like a long shadow in an alleyway, disappearing into the darkness.

The nearest pub had little to recommend it beyond the fact that it was the nearest pub, but that was all it needed to recommend it. That was enough.

My brother and The Undertaker stationed themselves at the bar and sat sampling the different whiskies that the bar served saying things like, 'a definite oaky undertone,' and 'a hint of toffee,' and 'a slow, mellow aftertaste,' and saying it all very seriously, as if they took the whole business very seriously, and nothing was more worthy of being taken seriously than identifying the different hints of flavour in different whiskies.

Ratty and the others were drinking beer and playing pool, and taking it all very seriously, as if drinking beer and playing pool were the most important things a person could possibly do. They were saying things like, 'Good shot!' and 'You bastard!' and 'Is that my pint?' and 'Your go.'

No one offered to buy me a drink. The Undertaker had forgotten about me. I sat apart and got as drunk as I possibly could by drinking what others had left behind, which probably isn't exactly what I would have chosen to do, if I had had a choice.

Others had left behind an array of drinks, and I was soon very drunk indeed, and had no clear perception of what was going on around me. I had only been drunk once or twice before and I wasn't too good at being drunk, to tell the truth.

It didn't take too long for the thought of the other people's drinks that I had been drinking – and the beer and pool being taken so seriously and the different hints of flavour in different whiskies – to make me feel sick. I rushed to the toilet.

I entered a cubicle and knelt down. I gripped the piss-soaked toilet seat and vomited the different hints of flavour in different whiskies, and the beer and pool being taken so seriously, and the other people's drinks that I had been drinking into the toilet bowl.

"Aaarrrggghhhhhh!" I vomited. "AAARRRGGGHHHH-HHHHH!"

It certainly wasn't my proudest moment. It didn't make me feel too great about myself.

After vomiting, I sat on the piss-soaked toilet seat and passed out with my head resting on my knees.

I awoke some time later with a jolt, feeling pretty miserable and pretty sore from the vomiting. I sat there for a few moments taking deep breaths and collecting myself, before leaving the vomit, and the cubicle, and the piss-soaked toilet seat in the past where they belonged.

I staggered back into the bar trying to look as if this was what I had planned all along.

My brother and his friends were nowhere to be seen. 'They probably forgot about me and went somewhere else,' I thought to myself, and it was a relief to be free of them. I felt free. It was a strange feeling, and reminded me of the past, like a smell that takes you back to your childhood.

I didn't know what else to do, so I sat at the bar and ordered a whisky, because it was a drink I knew the name of.

"Can I have a whisky, please?" I asked the barmaid as she walked past purposefully.

She turned to face me with a concerned frown. "Are you sure that's a good idea?" she said. I must have looked quite pale, or stank of vomit, or something.

"Yes, I think so," I said, trying, but probably failing, to sound sure of myself. Sounding sure of myself was a skill I hadn't developed, so I probably didn't sound too sure of myself at all.

She looked at me as if weighing up two sides of an argument. 'Well, on the one hand,' she might have thought, 'he looks rather pale and stinks of vomit. But on the other hand,' she might have continued thinking, weighing up the arguments, 'he is sitting upright and seems reasonably lucid.'

Eventually she decided in my favour.

I say, 'eventually' but it really didn't take her long. A few seconds was all it took.

"Which one would you like?" she asked.

"The cheapest, please," I said, wondering why there always had to be different types of things, and thinking of the money in my pocket that hadn't taken very long to count.

She laughed and picked a bottle from the shelf.

I felt an urge to talk to her, but I couldn't think of anything to say. I am not a great conversationalist if you must know the truth.

"Do you live round here?" I said, as she poured out the cheapest whisky, trying to make conversation. It was the best I could manage.

She seemed amused. "Um," she said, as if unsure whether to divulge any personal information. She probably thought I was going to follow her home or something. "Not too far away."

She didn't ask a follow-up question, or offer any more information, which is how conversations usually work. I was unsure how to proceed. I pondered my next move in silence.

"That'll be two pounds, please," she said.

I gave her the money and tried again as I did so.

"Have you worked here long?" I said quietly. It was the kind of question that someone who was trying to make conversation might reasonably ask.

"Um ..." she said, putting the money into the till. She was hardly even listening now; her mind was already on to the next thing. She was probably sick of pale-faced guys who stank of vomit trying, ineptly, to make conversation while ordering the cheapest whisky that money can buy.

"Excuse me," she said, and walked away.

I watched her walk away, like a passing car. Vroom, and she was gone.

I drank the cheapest whisky and grimaced. I didn't like whisky at the best of times, and this was certainly not the best of times.

I Find out the Truth

It didn't take Ratty long, eating wolfishly as he did, to finish his dessert. And once he had, he resumed his conversation with the gaunt ashen-faced man, even though the gaunt ashen-faced man, eating surgically as he did, had not yet finished his dessert.

Ratty was talking loudly, and despite the general din, I could hear almost every word that he said.

The gaunt ashen-faced man wasn't saying much because he was still performing surgery on his dessert. Ratty was doing all the talking. He was talking about me. Somehow, I just knew he was talking about me.

My body felt prickly like it was covered in pins.

"I met him once or twice," Ratty said, talking about me. "He's a fucking weirdo. I don't blame his brother for having nothing to do with him. I wouldn't have anything to do with him if he was my brother."

The gaunt ashen-faced man looked around with interest. "Is he here?" he said.

"Wouldn't have thought so," said Ratty, looking vaguely around the room. "They haven't spoken for years. As far as I know, they haven't spoken since before their mother died." He stopped as if he had remembered something. He had. "You know, he didn't even go to his own mother's funeral. That's the kind of person we're talking about."

The Warehouse Industry

It's true. I didn't go to my own mother's funeral. I was trying not to draw attention to myself. I had my reasons. Make of that what you will.

I am the kind of person who doesn't even go to his own mother's funeral. That's the kind of person I am.

"I met him on his brother's stag trip. We hired a boat for the weekend, and he came along," Ratty said, talking about me. "And he spent the whole weekend on his own, sitting apart, keeping himself to himself, looking fucking miserable. He didn't speak to anyone all weekend."

The gaunt ashen-faced man looked up and nodded to show that he was listening. He was still focused on his dessert and only looked up when he felt he needed to show that he was listening.

"Anyway, on the Saturday night, we went out for a drink or two," continued Ratty, winking for the gaunt man's benefit, but the gaunt man didn't see; he was focused on his dessert. "I don't think he had ever been drunk before, this was about twenty years ago, he was young, seventeen, eighteen, and he got wasted. I mean, really wasted. He lost it."

The gaunt ashen-faced man smiled wryly. He was the kind of man who never smiled unless it was wryly.

Ratty continued: "First of all, he got himself chucked out of a nightclub for molesting a girl while she was unconscious."

It's true. I've got no one but myself to blame. I did get myself chucked out of a nightclub for molesting a girl while she was unconscious.

I was going to tell you. I just haven't got round to it yet.

The thin pale woman, who was listening, flinched. It was barely perceptible, but she definitely flinched.

"Fuck!" said the gaunt ashen-faced man, whose eyebrows almost flew off his face. They took off and almost flew off his face. He now gave Ratty his full attention. His patient – the dessert – would just have to wait.

"We found him outside, unconscious, slumped in the doorway of a shop. Completely out of his head," said Ratty.

The gaunt ashen-faced man smiled a wry gaunt ashen smile. It was as if wry gaunt ashen smiles had been created just for him.

"And then," said Ratty, but his throat was blocked and he couldn't continue. He cleared his throat. Ahem.

"We woke him up, and he starts pushing his brother around, and screaming abuse at him, for no reason at all. He just snapped. He was like a wild animal."

Ratty spoke in short bursts because he was permanently short of breath. As far as breath was concerned he lived hand to mouth. He paused to have a sip of wine. He licked his lips. A drop escaped and dripped down his chin, disappearing inside a fold of flesh.

"Then he started swearing at random strangers in the fucking street. People were getting pissed off. It looked like it was going to get nasty."

The gaunt ashen-faced man widened his eyes to show that he thought that sort of behaviour quite beyond the pale. But he did it wryly as if life was just some sort of big joke.

"We had to pretty much carry him away after that."

"Fucking hell," said the gaunt ashen-faced man, who then allowed himself a wry smile. "What a nutter!"

"But he wasn't finished. On our way back to the boat. We were walking through a park. And there's a soldier, right, with his girlfriend, dressed in his full soldier's outfit, and it starts again. He can barely fucking stand, but he's calling this soldier all sorts of crazy fucking names. I can't even repeat some of the crazy fucking shit he came out with. And this soldier boy isn't too fucking happy, about being called whatever crazy shit he's getting called, and he says, 'If you don't shut the fuck up,' he says, 'I'm going to smash your fucking head in.' And he fucking means it too. But our boy isn't shutting up. Oh no. He just starts shouting louder and louder, like a fucking lunatic, all sorts of crazy shit. And this soldier, there's something in his eye, or something not in his eye. So the soldier lays into him, starts beating the shit out of him, and I mean really kicking and beating the shit out of him, smashing his head in, as he said he would, and our boy's lying there on the ground, getting the shit kicked out of him, and, weirdly, he's not making a sound, not a single fucking sound."

"What!" said the gaunt ashen-faced man as if he just couldn't believe what he was hearing. "Fucking weirdo."

Ratty took a moment for a deep breath and sip of wine. The gaunt ashen-faced man waited patiently for the conclusion of the story.

"And then what?" said the gaunt ashen-faced man when his patience had run out.

"Eventually, the soldier wore himself out, and fucked off, and left him lying there motionless on the ground."

My body turned to ice, but I was burning inside. I felt light and heavy at the same time. I held onto the table as if worried I might float away. I could hear voices all around me, but I had no way of knowing who they belonged to or what they were saying, or if they were real or not.

"We carried him back to the boat, but he refused to go inside. He crawled up onto the roof and lay down, and that was it. He passed out."

This was not the version of events I had been led to believe. I felt like I was expanding; like I was getting larger and larger or everyone else was getting smaller and smaller. I gripped the table as tightly as I could.

"Anyway, it was almost dawn and we decided to play a little joke on him."

A little joke.

The gaunt ashen-faced man smiled. And it was a wry gaunt ashen smile. It was a smile that suggested he knew a thing or two about playing little jokes on people.

I was sinking. I imagined that I had lost control of my face and that my features were floating around randomly.

Ratty paused to take a few deep breaths.

"Well, we'd been up drinking all night, and it seemed like a good idea. You know what it's like." The gaunt man nodded. "We thought it would be funny.

"Just before dawn, we started the motor, and cruised off downriver. We stopped at a quiet spot by some fields. There was no one around. Everyone else had gone to sleep, apart from me and Peter," he gestured towards The Undertaker, who was chatting amiably to someone or other.

Peter: so that was his real name. The Undertaker was called Peter.

"We woke him up, which wasn't easy. He was completely disorientated. He looked around with a look of wild, blind panic. He made as if to get up, as if he was going to hurl himself into the water, or make a run for it. He was making these wild grunting sounds. We had to restrain him, or he'd have drowned himself."

The gaunt man's gaunt eyebrows prepared for take-off.

"He was growling at us and gnashing his teeth, like a fucking animal. The boy was gone. It was actually pretty scary. Then Peter looks at him with deadly seriousness and says, 'Look mate, I would advise you to shut the fuck up and calm down. Someone's going to be out looking for you, and if you get caught you're going down for a long fucking time.' The boy stopped growling and gnashing his teeth, and gave us a wild panicked look. He didn't know what the hell was going on. And then Pete tells him: 'You fucking killed someone last night, you psycho!'"

I remembered that. I'll remember that until my dying day. If I remember one thing as I lie on my deathbed, it will probably be The Undertaker telling me that I'd fucking killed someone. It's hard to forget something like that.

The gaunt ashen-faced man arranged his features, somehow, into a quizzical expression. "And he believed you?" he asked, as if nothing in the world could matter less.

"We told him what had supposedly happened," replied Ratty. "He remembered nothing. We told him that after the soldier had kicked the shit out of him in the park, he had grabbed a large rock and beaten him to death with it in a bloody frenzy. We told him that he had dragged the body into some undergrowth, and covered it with leaves and dirt, and that someone would find it, sooner rather than later.

"He looked at us in disbelief. But then he looked at his hands, front and back."

Ratty was acting it out as he spoke. He looked at his own fleshy hands, front and back. "And he saw the blood and the broken skin.

"He felt his face." And Ratty felt his own fleshy face. "And felt the soreness and the bruises."

"He looked at his shirt." And Ratty looked down at his shirt, bespattered with evidence of the feast he had just enjoyed. "And saw that it was ripped and stained with blood. And he muttered something quietly to himself." Ratty paused for a sip of wine. A drop escaped his mouth and dripped down his chin. He wiped it away with the back of his hand. "He believed us, all right."

The gaunt ashen-faced man smiled one of his famous wry ashen smiles, the ones that had been created just for him, and I almost hated him for it.

"We told him to keep out of sight for the rest of the day, and to never speak to anyone about what had happened. Especially not his fucking brother."

I felt like bits of me were disintegrating. I gripped the table as tightly as I could, as if that might help, somehow.

"And did his brother ever find out?" asked the gaunt ashen-faced man.

"I think Peter told him, eventually," Ratty replied disinterestedly, as if he had lost interest in his own story now that it had reached its conclusion. "At least he said he was going to. I don't know if he actually did or not."

I had no idea what to do. All I could perceive was a fleshy mass that I knew as Ratty. My head was spinning. Everything else was blurred and indistinct.

A glass chimed purposefully from somewhere outside of what was happening to me, from somewhere that was blurred and indistinct, and had nothing to do with me at all.

I gripped the table as tightly as I could; gripping the table as tightly as I could was all I had left. It was my only hope.

Part Four

A Fine Sunny Morning

It was a fine sunny morning. The sky was clear and blue. It was an unusually fine spell of weather we were having.

I had a feeling that it was going to be a good day. It felt as though there was change in the air. The owner had arrived again that morning, which was a good sign: a good shiny expensive-looking sign.

I had become fixated on being made redundant from the warehouse, as if being made redundant from the warehouse was the greatest thing that could possibly happen to a person.

So, I stood around with my feeling that it was going to be a good day, and the change in the air, and waited to be made redundant. I was so excited that it was hard to concentrate on the mundane tasks that usually occupied my time at the warehouse. I usually didn't mind the mundane tasks that filled my time at the warehouse. They kept me occupied, at least. But today, I couldn't concentrate. I was too excited about being made redundant.

Eventually – because when you're excited time stretches itself out and has a lie down – the phone rang. I picked it up but I didn't say hello. I was too excited to bother about such mundane things as saying hello.

For a moment there was nothing in the world but a crackly silence. In those days, some of the silences were crackly, but you don't really have crackly silences anymore, do you?

"Are you there?" whispered the manager's daughter, as if there was someone behind her.

"Yes," I answered. "I'm here."

"OK, I'm coming down." She put the phone down and within seconds I heard the sound of high-heeled shoes clattering hurriedly down the exterior metallic skeletal staircase.

Soon she was standing breathlessly before me. She looked at me strangely, as if she was trying to work out something that puzzled her.

She fiddled with the various items carelessly arranged on the counter in the warehouse. The tools of my trade.

There was a moment of silence between us, and for that moment there was nothing else in the world.

"You don't talk much, do you?" she said.

"No, I guess not. No I don't," I replied, not really knowing how to reply. I never really know what to say when people state the obvious, which people seem to do quite often.

She contemplated me. "Do I scare you?" she asked with a girlish smile.

"No, not at all," I answered, and it was the truth. She didn't. She was one of the only people I had ever met who didn't scare me at all. I'm not sure why. "I guess I just don't have a lot to say," I continued. She seemed a little disappointed.

"Oh, I see," she said absently, as if she didn't really see at all. "Are you happy not having a lot to say? I can't imagine I'd be happy if I didn't have a lot to say."

"I'm not really sure," I said, which was the truth. I was pretty sure that I wasn't too happy not having a lot to say, but I couldn't be sure.

"Oh, OK," said the manager's daughter, absently fiddling with a small, handheld device that was used to speedily administer adhesive tape to packages of all shapes and sizes, and was an indispensable tool to the warehouse worker.

She stopped fiddling and contemplated me again. "It's just that I think I like you, but I'm not sure why. You never talk. You've never told me a single thing about yourself."

Her tone had changed; she was suddenly very much present. She skipped over to me. Her face was only inches from mine.

"Maybe that's why I think I like you. You're a mystery." She spoke slowly and quietly now, her face so close to mine that I could smell the coffee on her breath, which is not a very original thing to be able to smell on someone's breath, but is, at least, plausible. She looked into my eyes and laughed.

"They're going to be calling you in soon," she said, in the manner of someone who is privy to inside information. "But you're not leaving. You'll be better off staying here, anyway. I could get you a promotion. How does 'warehouse manager' sound?"

It didn't sound too great to tell the truth.

"I'm not sure," I said, because I didn't know what else to say, and I didn't want to hurt her feelings; it was a kind offer, or at least it was trying to be a kind offer.

"Anyway, you're not leaving," she told me. "You're definitely not leaving."

The Phone Rings Again

A few hours later the phone rang again. I picked up the receiver but I didn't say anything. Nor did the manager's daughter who was on the other end of the line.

There was a brief, crackly silence that for the briefest of moments was the only thing that happened in the world.

Then:

"They'll see you now," said the manager's daughter curtly, as if nothing at all made any difference to her whatsoever.

Upstairs, she was busily typing away at a computer, as if she had a long list of things to do that all involved typing away at a computer.

"Ah, good afternoon," she said formally, as if I was just another person that she had never seen before. "If you wouldn't mind taking a seat the owner will see you shortly."

I sat down and looked around the room for something to do. There was a table with a few well-thumbed magazines placed neatly upon it, which were all aimed at particular groups of people, such as people who like cars, or people who like watching TV, or people who like nature, or people who are women. But none of them were aimed at people like me.

I didn't even know if there were people like me.

After a few minutes had worn themselves out, the manager poked his screwed-up little face out of the 'meeting room'. I'm not sure if I've mentioned already that the manager had a face that was screwed-up like a raisin, and that his face was on the small side in proportion to the rest of his body.

"You can show him in now," said the manager. He was speaking to his daughter, as if speaking directly to me was beneath him. "And we'll have two coffees as well. Soon as you can," he added, as an afterthought. He was the kind of person who never missed an opportunity to tell people what to do.

"The owner will see you now," said the manager's daughter blandly, as if I was just another face that she had never seen before, and meant absolutely nothing to her whatsoever.

"Thank you," I replied politely, playing along as best I could, which wasn't very well.

I entered the 'meeting room' warily, despite my great excitement, which had not lessoned. Every single bit of me was excited. I could think of no greater thing that could happen to me than being made redundant. Imagine the excitement! But still I was wary.

"Sit down, please," the owner said affably. He could afford to be affable. He was the owner.

I sat down carefully, as if my excitement was a fragile thing that could easily break.

"Fine weather we're having, isn't it?" said the owner.

"Yes. Fine," I replied, not really sure how else to respond to such a banal observation.

Seeing that I was someone not really much given to small talk, the owner decided that it was time to get down to business, and looked at me over the rim of his glasses to show that he was getting down to business. That was the kind of owner he was: the kind of owner that looked at you over the rim of his glasses to show that he was getting down to business.

"Now, it had been our intention today to ask you if you would be willing to take voluntary redundancy," said the owner. I nodded eagerly. The owner took a deep breath. "But, it would appear that no more redundancies are, in fact, necessary." He smiled affably, as if this was terribly good news, which it wasn't, and he expected me to be terribly pleased, which I wasn't.

"Besides which," he continued, looking down and shuffling his papers, as if what he wanted to say was written down somewhere, "I hear that you work wonders downstairs, and that you are a nigh on indispensable member of staff. Indispensable. Yes, I'm pretty sure that was the word. Indispensable."

The owner looked at the manager – who was keeping himself busy by scowling at me – as if seeking confirmation of my indispensability.

The manager coughed unnecessarily. "Yes, no, absolutely," he said. "Very good." Cough. "Indispensable."

His daughter had made him say it. This was her way of ensuring that I stay, of ensuring that she wasn't totally abandoned.

'She must be blackmailing him,' I thought. 'She must know something about him that he doesn't want anyone else to know.'

I noticed damp patches under the manager's arms. He was clearly uncomfortable.

The owner smiled at me again, as if he expected me to be pleased. But I wasn't pleased and he seemed confused, as if he couldn't understand why I wasn't pleased. As far as he was concerned, I should have been pleased. He could not think of a single reason why I shouldn't be pleased. Despite his confusion, he persevered. He was a consummate professional. "So, we just wanted to thank you," he said, "for your efforts, and assure you that your job here is safe." He sat back and folded his arms. "At least for the time being," he added, as an afterthought, to cover himself.

I could see that he was expecting some sort of expression of relief or gratitude, but I was in no way able to give him what he was expecting. I felt no relief or gratitude, no relief or gratitude at all. I couldn't quite believe what had happened. I was stunned. I had not even for a moment considered the possibility of not being made redundant. Not being made redundant was not even a possibility in my mind. Redundancy was my only hope. It was my great excitement.

I felt that feeling that you get when you realise that something you were really excited about is not going to happen, which for a moment is quite an exciting feeling in itself. It opens up its own possibilities. It has its advantages.

There was a moment when no one spoke; it was a moment when anything might have happened. Anything might have happened, but nothing did; we all just sat there, not saying or doing anything.

"OK?" said the owner, after the moment had passed, trying to bring the meeting to a close.

"OK," I replied, standing up.

"Well, thank you again," said the owner, standing up and offering me his hand to shake, which I pretended not to notice.

"Thanks," I said, for some reason, as I turned away and walked out of the room.

On my way out the manager's daughter flashed me a smug, self-satisfied smile. Her earlier pretence had been abandoned. She knew me again now.

"I hope everything went well," she said, knowingly, and laughed.

I looked at her but didn't say anything; I didn't really know what to say to her. I was still adjusting to the reality of not being made redundant, and I wasn't in the mood to think of things to say to the manager's daughter.

An Advert for the Only Nightclub in Town

I don't think I made any particular effort to find my brother and his friends that night, but I found them nonetheless.

I found them in what seemed to be the town's only nightclub. I saw them through the window. They were on display.

There seemed to be only one nightclub in the whole town, and it had large shopfront windows. At the only nightclub in town, nothing was left to the imagination.

My brother and his friends were on display in the large shopfront windows, as if they were an advert for the only nightclub in town.

The Line Moved Slowly

It was the kind of perfectly ordinary market town where, on a typical day, nothing out of the ordinary ever happened. But, for some reason, this wasn't a typical day.

A line of people waited to enter the nightclub, and as they did so they were able to look through the large shopfront windows and see what they were missing. They didn't have to imagine what they were missing, because they could see what they were missing through the large shopfront windows.

The line moved slowly, and was regulated by a surly man dressed in black. The man seemed to enjoy his job in his own surly way. I guess that's just how some people enjoy things.

I can't imagine why, but I went and stood at the back of the line. I guess there was nothing else for me to do, so I didn't really have a choice. I had to do something. Doing nothing wasn't really an option, and I couldn't think of anything else to do.

I watched my brother and his friends through the large shopfront windows. They had ended up in the only nightclub in town because it was the only nightclub in town. They didn't really have a choice either.

The line moved slowly.

There were two girls in front of me. They were talking about what arseholes their boyfriends were, or what a bastard so-and-so was, or whatever else you would expect them to be talking about. They are not convincing three-dimensional characters. They are just story fodder, so it doesn't really matter what they were talking about.

I looked down and examined their bare legs and stilettoed feet, which gave me a sort of woozy feeling.

There was no real need for the line to move so slowly. Anyone who spared the time to look through its large shopfront windows could see that the nightclub was half empty.

I waited in line. You may, understandably, wonder why; but I had nowhere else to go and nothing else to do, so I didn't really have a choice. That's why.

No one ever really has a choice, but that's a moot point.

The line moved slowly.

A Speech

I heard the chiming of a glass from somewhere outside of what was happening to me. Somewhere blurred and indistinct that had nothing to do with me at all.

The chiming was caused by the man I recognised as The Undertaker – Peter - tapping the rim of a wine glass with a piece of cutlery. Everyone understood that this meant he was trying to draw attention to himself so that he might say a few words, as was customary on such occasions.

I gripped the table tightly as if it was the only thing keeping me afloat, or the only thing holding me down. It was my only hope, gripping the table, it was all I had left in the world.

A hushed, expectant silence settled over the room. Everyone turned to look at The Undertaker, my brother's best man, who as custom dictated, was about to make a speech.

He started talking, confidently gesticulating as he spoke, like a man who felt comfortable in his own skin, no matter how bloated it had become over the years.

"I've known this man," said The Undertaker, gesturing towards my brother, "since we were this high." The Undertaker placed his hand about four feet from the ground indicating that he had known my brother since the two of them were small children.

He paused for comic effect.

"And he couldn't handle his drink then either!" It was a bad joke, but people still laughed. They knew what was expected of them. A wedding is not the time to not laugh at bad jokes.

The Undertaker allowed the corners of his mouth to turn upwards slightly, as if he couldn't think of a single reason why he shouldn't allow the corners of his mouth to turn upwards slightly.

He continued making his speech, constructing it word by word, and sentence by sentence.

"And, of course, this isn't the first time I've been his best man." He paused to allow a few people to snigger knowingly, as if getting married more than once was some sort of private joke. "But I hope that it's the last, because this young lady," he looked at my brother's bride, "is just lovely."

Everyone smiled as expected, because they knew what was expected of them. "Oooohhh," said some people. "Aaaahhhh," said others, doing what was expected of them. Some people applauded; others whooped and cheered. The room was united in appreciation of my brother's bride's loveliness, as was right and fitting in the circumstances.

The Undertaker continued, counting on his fingers: "She's beautiful, funny, kind, thoughtful, talented, sweet, caring, passionate …" He trailed off. There were a few knowing titters; The Undertaker paused. "I wouldn't mind marrying her myself!"

The Undertaker's jokes were like nails in a coffin, and were delivered with solemn gravity, but everyone still laughed as expected. A wedding is not the time to not laugh at jokes just because they are like nails in a coffin and are delivered with solemn gravity.

I didn't laugh, but was surrounded by the laughter of others nonetheless. It didn't matter whether I laughed or not, I was still surrounded by the laughter of others nonetheless.

I imagine The Undertaker thought he had his audience in the palm of his hand. 'I've got this lot in the palm of my hand,' I imagine he thought.

"Anyway," continued The Undertaker, "as I say, he really can't handle his drink. I remember on his first stag trip, we were in a nightclub, and he got so drunk he passed out on the dance floor."

Laughs.

"While he was dancing!"

More laughs; bellier laughs. Some particularly excitable people might have slapped their thighs, but I can't be sure. It was all I could do to focus on The Undertaker and the contents of the speech he was making.

My brother managed to smile indulgently, but I imagine that inside he wasn't too pleased. One of his eyes might have twitched slightly, which would have been a clue. But if his eye did twitch, I didn't notice, or couldn't see from where I was sitting.

"But the less said about his first stag trip the better," continued The Undertaker. Peter. I can't quite get used to that. "It probably wasn't our finest hour. But don't worry, it was much more civilised this time, I can assure you. He's a changed man."

I couldn't take anymore. I closed my eyes and concentrated on gripping the table as tightly as I could, which was quite tightly. The Undertaker continued making his speech, working his way through three or four well-rehearsed anecdotes that all seemed to involve my brother getting drunk and making a fool of himself in some way, as was appropriate. And I might have gained some pleasure from listening to them had I not been using all my energy trying to stay afloat, and gripping the table as tightly as I could.

He ended his speech with a toast, which was what he was expected to end his speech with. He composed himself, and adopted the kind of grave expression that he might usually have reserved for the bereaved relatives of the recently deceased.

"Here's to the happy couple," he said, raising his glass. "And let's hope the second marriage lasts longer than the first!" That sentiment won a big cheer from his audience. The wedding guests stood and raised their glasses as one. Everyone seemed to know what to do, somehow.

"To the happy couple," said everyone, or something like that, and sat down, knowing what to do.

I neither stood nor raised a glass. I was gripping the table tightly, as if nothing else mattered. If it was possible, which I don't think it was, I might even have tightened my grip.

Time to Leave

The meal over, people began to drift off. The table emptied. The little girl ran off to find other people to whom life was still a mystery.

The thin pale woman stared blankly ahead at nothing as she helped Ratty to his feet. Once upright, he waved at The Undertaker and gave him the thumbs up. If he had been a younger leaner man he might have walked over to him and exchanged a few words, but he wasn't a younger leaner man, he was an older larger man, so he didn't.

Instead, he waddled off to find somewhere else to sit, accompanied by the thin pale woman, who must have done something terrible to deserve such a fate. But it doesn't really matter whether she did or not: she's only story fodder. This story is not about the thin pale woman. You don't need to know whether or not she did something terrible to deserve such a fate.

I was still gripping the table tightly. The speeches were over and I was soon sitting alone at the table, but still I gripped it tightly, as if it was the only thing keeping me afloat or the only thing stopping me from floating away.

I knew I had to leave, or people would begin to notice me sitting alone at the table and gripping it as tightly as I could. And then someone would probably approach me and say something like, 'Are you all right?' or 'Can I help you?' and I couldn't possibly allow that to happen.

It was time to leave.

I stood up and was actually surprised to discover that my legs still worked. I genuinely hadn't expected them to still be working.

I left. I stumbled towards fresh air. I almost felt pleased with myself. I had done well. It had been a struggle but I had done well, and a new world awaited. A new world where I knew the truth.

In I Go

The line moved slowly. But it was definitely moving. I really don't want to go into the nightclub, but inevitably I must. I would make the line move slower if I could, but I can't; or I would stop it moving altogether if it was within my power, but it isn't. There is absolutely nothing I can do to change the speed at which the line is moving. Nothing at all. It's not true that nothing's inevitable: the past is inevitable. And some of the future is too.

The line moved slowly.

The two girls in front of me reached the front of the line. The surly bouncer surveyed them lewdly from head to foot, and from foot to head, and temporarily discarded his trademark surliness.

"In you go, girls," he said, with a leer, watching them disappear into the press of bodies inside. "Behave yourselves," he said to their behinds.

I was at the front of the line. That means that whether I want to or not – and I don't – I am about to enter the nightclub.

The bouncer looked at me surlily. Under his gaze, I wilted. I felt a little unsteady on my feet. I swayed a little, drunkenly.

I steadied myself.

"How old are you, mate?" said the bouncer.

"I'm twenty-two," I lied, thinking that a lie was more convincing than the truth. I was eighteen. There was no need to lie, I was old enough to enter the nightclub, but I thought a lie was more convincing than the truth.

"Got any ID?" he said, suspiciously. I couldn't really blame him for being suspicious. I was lying after all.

"No," I said, trying to act as if it made no difference whatsoever, and I wasn't bothered anyway, which was how I thought it was best to act in the circumstances.

He examined me.

"You're drunk," he said, as if he had arrived at this conclusion after a series of complex deductions.

"Not really," I slurred in response. "I've only had a couple."

"A couple of what? Pints of whisky?" He snorted. He had amused himself. He thought himself witty in his own surly way. He looked around to see if there was anyone else to find this funny, but there wasn't.

"Couple of pints," I said, with only my scattered wits to guide me.

There was a pause while he considered me. I didn't hold out much hope that he would let me in. Little did I know that he would, inevitably, let me in.

"Can you stand up straight?" he asked. He was interrogating me, testing my fitness to enter the nightclub. If you were to enter the nightclub you had to be able to stand up straight, or else you might fall over and then what would happen? Chaos, probably.

I did my best impression of standing up straight, which I thought was quite good. The bouncer seemed to agree. He moved onto the next question.

"Have you got any money?" he asked.

I tapped my pocket. There was a slight but audible sound of coins jingling. They didn't amount to much, as you know, but he seemed satisfied.

"OK," the bouncer said warily, and sighed. He patted me down, in the style of someone who takes no pleasure in patting other men down, but does it for the common good.

"In you go then," he said. He looked at me as if he thought he might one day rue his decision.

"Thank you," I said, for some reason, as if I had anything to thank him for.

I tried to walk casually into the nightclub, but I had trouble opening the door, which was closed. I struggled with it for a few seconds before the surly bouncer came to my aid.

"Turn the handle," said the bouncer behind me, as if he couldn't believe how stupid I was, which he probably couldn't.

I turned the handle and, to my relief, the door opened.

"Fucking hell," said the bouncer, behind my back.

I entered the nightclub.

In I go.

Nightclubbing

Inside the nightclub there was cheap mass-produced music everywhere: it was lying in congealing, sticky puddles on the floor and dripping, like condensed sweat, from the ceiling. It pounded at my brain with its invisible metaphorical fists.

The nightclub had an unloved look about it. It seemed that very little care or thought had been devoted to its decoration. The walls were plain and bare with only one or two posters near the bar to break up the barren monotony of its featurelessness.

One of the posters was an advert for a new brand of alcoholic drink and consisted of a picture of a rounded bottle containing a noxious-looking green liquid set against a black background. There were letters above and below the picture, which were arranged like this:

NEW! TOXIC NEW!

(picture)

CAN YOU HANDLE IT?

I didn't find the advertisement terribly appealing and I wondered what kind of person would.

I looked around the nightclub. It was small enough so that from where I was standing it could easily be looked around without too much difficulty.

I noticed my brother on the dance floor; his eyes were shut tight as if he was determined not to acknowledge the existence of anything else in the world.

I noticed The Undertaker talking solemnly with a man at the bar. The man at the bar had a face that looked as though it would brook no nonsense and he was talking volubly. It seemed that he was doing most of the talking and that The Undertaker was doing most of the listening. The Undertaker nodded vigorously every so often to show that he was listening intently. He was a good listener; being a good listener is one of the skills a good undertaker prides himself on.

Ratty was there too, his arm around a girl in a dark dress. He was shouting into her ear, straining to make himself heard above the music, and every so often he pulled away to see her reaction to something he said, and every time the girl in the dark dress tried to please him with her reaction by smiling or laughing or looking surprised, or whatever reaction was appropriate. I don't know why she was trying to please him, and I wondered what reason she could possibly have for wanting to please him.

I walked over to The Undertaker. He was my only hope. I had little or no money. The jingle in my pocket had been just for show. It didn't amount to much. The Undertaker was my only hope so I didn't really have a choice.

I went and stood right next to him at the bar, but he was so engrossed in whatever the other man had to say that he was totally oblivious to the fact that I was standing right next to him at the bar.

I tapped him clumsily on the shoulder, but he thought that someone had just clumsily bumped into him and so continued not to notice me. I called out to him, but he was listening so intently to the words that came out of the other man's face that he was deaf to all other sounds, or at least he was deaf to the sound of me calling out to him. I began to suspect that there was nothing I could do to induce him to take any notice of me.

I began to feel utterly forsaken. I wondered why I struggled so pathetically with things other people found so easy, or didn't even have to think about, like attracting someone's attention when they are standing right next to you at the bar.

But then I had a stroke of luck. The other man's attention was distracted by an acquaintance that appeared on his other side, and was able to attract his attention with no trouble or failed attempts at all. The Undertaker, freed from the chains of conversation, at least momentarily, looked around and saw me pathetically standing right next to him.

"You all right, mate," he said, but it wasn't a question, it was his manner of greeting someone. "I thought we'd lost you there."

"I think I passed out in the toilet," I replied, shouting, because every time I tried to move closer to him he backed away as if I had foul breath, which I most probably did. "But I'm OK now," I continued, as if anyone cared.

"You found us all right then?" he said, smirking, though I wasn't sure why.

"It was the only place still open," I said, trying my hardest to have a conversation.

"Oh," said The Undertaker not even bothering to feign interest. He took a sip of his drink. This reminded me.

"Can you buy me a drink?" I said, pathetically. He didn't reply immediately. "I've got no money left," I explained. "I'll pay you back."

"OK," he said with perceptible reluctance, after reluctantly considering my request. "What do you want?"

"A double whisky, please." I was beginning to understand how these things worked.

"I'll get you a single," said The Undertaker. He turned back to the bar. He didn't talk to me or even look at me as he waited to get served. It took all his concentration to wait to get served.

By the time the drink arrived, the other man was ready to start talking again, and had started talking again. The Undertaker passed me the drink he had bought me absently, his attention already elsewhere.

"Thanks," I said. I was genuinely grateful. I had come to view The Undertaker as my only friend in the world: a distracted and distant only friend in the world admittedly, but an only friend in the world nonetheless. And when you're desperate and pathetic, like I was, you take what you can get. You can't afford to be fussy when you're desperate and pathetic like I was.

But The Undertaker didn't hear my expression of genuine, pathetic gratitude. He was listening intently, by that point, to the man whose face looked as though it would brook no nonsense, which seemed to take all of his concentration, so that he had none left to hear my expression of pathetic gratitude.

I took a sip of whisky and grimaced, but perhaps it was a little less of a grimace than earlier. I was getting used to the taste of whisky, and was beginning to think that, maybe, it wasn't too bad after all. I looked around and considered my options. There weren't too many to tell the truth.

I opted for a worn out black leather sofa which occupied a corner of the room and had a neglected air about it. I probably felt sorry for it or something, as if the worn out sofa could care less about whether I felt sorry for it or not, or was a thing that was worth feeling sorry for at all.

"Thanks," I said again, pathetically, in the direction of The Undertaker before walking off. He didn't seem to notice. He had forsaken me.

I went and sat on the worn out black leather sofa. It really was worn out; it was covered with rips and scars. You could tell it had been through some tough times; you could tell it had had a hard life. If I had felt sorry for it before, I felt even more sorry for it now, whether or not it was a thing worth feeling sorry for at all.

The sofa sagged without resistance under my weight, as if it had resigned itself to no longer being able to offer resistance a long time ago.

Nevertheless, the sofa was comfortable in its own worn out kind of way. It was a worn out kind of comfort; the kind of comfort that had nothing left to give. I sipped my whisky and grimaced. I looked around. I was surrounded by a forest of legs. I sat, sunken on the worn out sofa, sipping my drink slowly, trying to make it last as long as I possibly could, and hoping that no one would notice.

No one did. Time passed. The forest swayed in the wind, which was music.

It was later in the evening when I noticed Ratty sauntering out of the toilet, which was right next to the worn out sofa. As he sauntered, he was buttoning up his trousers and looking particularly pleased with himself. Ratty was the kind of person who always looked pleased with himself. But, as he sauntered out of the toilet, he was looking particularly pleased with himself.

Following in his wake was a petite pale-faced girl with smudged make up and tousled hair. It was the girl in the dark dress that I had seen him shouting in the ear of earlier.

As she followed in his wake, the girl wiped her mouth with the back of her hand. Her eyes were almost closed; I wondered how she could see anything out of them at all. She looked hopelessly drunk and staggered unsteadily. She fell back on the wall for support. If the wall hadn't been there she probably would have fallen over.

I watched her avidly as she felt her way along the wall towards me and the worn out black leather sofa. The worn out black leather sofa and I. We were a team now.

The wall was acting as her guide and support, her only friend in this hour of need. She could barely stand. I thought about getting up and helping her to a seat, but I didn't. To tell the truth, I probably wouldn't have been much help anyway. I've never really been much help to anyone if you want to know the truth.

Eventually, she reached the sofa and collapsed onto it, succumbing with a jolt to its worn out embrace. She hadn't appeared to notice me and certainly didn't acknowledge my presence; she sat down out of urgent necessity rather than because she had noticed me.

As soon as she was sat down she passed out; she was worn out, like the sofa.

Her unconscious presence excited me, which was something beyond my control. I couldn't control the fact that her unconscious presence excited me. It wasn't my fault. It was an uncontrollable sense of excitement.

I imagined that she had chosen to sit next to me, rather than it being an act of unconscious necessity, as if, in her hour of need, she had sought me out because I was the one best placed to offer her comfort. I felt that I had been called upon; that, somehow, it was my duty to offer her comfort, as if offering her comfort was the only decent thing to do. But still I didn't know how; I had no idea how to offer her comfort. I honestly couldn't remember ever having offered anyone comfort before. Not that I wouldn't have wanted to, but surely because the opportunity had just never arisen. But now the opportunity had arisen. The opportunity had unconsciously collapsed on the worn out sofa right next to me, and was waiting for me to offer it some sort of comfort. But still I wasn't sure how.

The worn out sofa came to my aid. We were a team, like I said, and it had deteriorated in such a way that - at the moment when I most needed some help and guidance - the pale-faced girl slumped a little towards me and her delicate, egg-shaped head came to rest very gently, on my shoulder. I imagined that I was offering her comfort, that I was supporting her in her hour of need.

My excitement grew. It grew almost to a thrill. My whole body tingled with excitement. Up close her beauty was breathtaking; it was almost unbelievable that such beauty could exist in such drab and loveless surroundings. It made me think that there had to be something very wrong with the world.

'There is definitely something very wrong in the world,' I thought, 'for such a creature to be slumped next to me on this worn out sofa, in this drab and loveless place, in such need of comfort.'

There was something not quite right about the whole thing.

The sofa gave way beneath her. It offered no resistance, and provided no support. And as the sofa gave way, so she leaned into me further and further, her unconscious body unable to support itself. I sat there awkwardly, wanting to offer comfort but not knowing how. I had only instinct to guide me: dulled, drunken instinct. Not that that makes it all right.

I put my arm around her. What else could I have done? I wanted to do the right thing; I wanted to offer her comfort, and putting my arm around her was the only way I knew how. She slumped further into me, and I was able to imagine that she was nestling into me, that she was finding comfort, and being comforted by me. I felt good; I managed to convince myself that I was doing a good thing; a thing that she, at some future time, might feasibly thank me for.

I rested my hand on the bare flesh of her arm. It was unfathomably soft; it was cool, and ever so slightly damp. There is nothing I could compare it to; it was incomparable. It was the softest, most beautiful thing I had ever felt. It was hard to understand how such beauty, such a sensation, could exist in such a world. It was a thing I could in no way understand. I closed my eyes as if that would help me make some sort of sense of it all, but it didn't. It didn't help me make any sort of sense of it all. I had only instinct to guide me; dulled, drunken instinct and the worn out sofa, which duly obliged me by sagging a little more under the weight of the pale-faced girl so that she had no choice but to succumb decisively to my embrace.

I rubbed her arm tenderly, as if rubbing her arm was absolutely the right thing to do in the circumstances, and I shifted my position so that she nestled a little more snugly into me. Her flesh was cool and wonderful. Her flesh was the most wonderful thing I had ever known. I had never known wonder like it.

We sat there like that for a while. For those blissful few moments, I imagined myself doing a good thing, offering comfort to someone in sore need of comfort, to someone whose beauty and delicacy could not simply be abandoned to the whims of a world they were too beautiful and delicate for. And we might have sat there like that a while longer, without any trouble at all, had not my eyes fell to examining her exposed legs, her helplessly splayed feet, and the mounds of her breasts which disappeared provocatively beneath the protective fabric of her black dress. Even in the drab darkness of the loveless nightclub, at such close quarters I could see the soft, downy, almost invisible hairs that covered them, like fine grass on a distant hillside, and that only served to make them more alluring.

I was carried away. I was no more in control than the river that flows, or the wind that blows, or the grass that grows. I couldn't stop myself, I really couldn't.

But I knew it was no good I was up to, like a flood, or a storm, or an overgrown garden. It was no good. I knew that. I know that.

I looked around. No one was paying us any attention. There was something about the lowly position of the worn out sofa that leant itself to not being noticed. Again, the worn out sofa had come to my aid. The worn out sofa was my accomplice. It was on my side. The coast was clear. It was like I had this wonderful view all to myself with no one else around to spoil it.

I shifted position, and she slumped forward with a jerk, so that her head almost came to rest on my thigh. I lifted her up and folded myself around her, as if shielding her from something she really shouldn't see, as if I was doing her a favour, which was not what I was doing her at all.

She was more beautiful than anything I had ever seen. I couldn't understand how such beauty could possibly exist.

I'm not trying to make excuses; I'm trying to explain. There is a difference. At least I think there's a difference.

With my left arm still around her shoulders, I stroked her thigh with my right. My touches were gentle, tender, loving. I was an affectionate lover, or at least I would have been.

I ascended into a celestial realm of pleasure. It was untold pleasure; it was unheard of pleasure. I had no idea that such pleasure existed, or could possibly exist. It was unthinkable. The feeling was surprising and magical, like dawn when you're young. I could have stroked her thigh for eternity, but there was her neck just waiting to be kissed. I bent over and started kissing her neck. It felt like a secret place that no one else knew about. It tasted slightly of sweat, but I had never tasted anything so delicious. Forbidden fruit. I kissed her lips, which were parted slightly and felt soft and buoyant. I bit her lower lip gently. She seemed to moan, almost imperceptibly. Meanwhile, I ran my fingers through her hair. We were lovers in a clinch, or at least I was. We were like those lovers you see in old paintings, or at least I was. It was divine, immortal, unheard of. I was insensible to everything else in the world. For a moment the entire world was only comprised of beauty, and pleasure, and comfort, and there was nothing else. I held her head in my arms, like I was protecting her, which was not what I was doing at all.

    I returned to her thigh. Her immortal thigh. I moved up, up, up towards her breasts. I had been saving myself. I pressed myself against her.

    Hate me if you want to, I deserve it. I've only got myself to blame.

A Darkness

Somehow, I became aware of a darkness falling over me, like the shadow of a cloud.

I froze. For a moment I remained dead still. Pleasure turned to panic.

"What the fuck do you think you're doing?" said an angry female voice, and I knew it was talking to me.

I had no idea how to reply. What did I think I was I doing? I had no idea. It had started with me thinking I was trying to offer someone comfort, but that was no longer what I was doing. I had moved on from trying to offer comfort, and now I could think of no words to describe what I was trying to do.

I suddenly felt very sick. I was drunk, remember, and young and foolish. I was hopelessly naive. I wasn't used to being drunk, and couldn't handle my drink, which is a thing people say. There was something inside me. It needed to come out. It was sick. I was going to be sick.

The Dark End of the Street

"What the fuck do you think you're doing?" said the angry female voice again, because I hadn't answered or responded in any way at all the first time she had asked, and she wanted an answer.

The voice was shrill and angry, and I couldn't blame it. It had every reason to be shrill and angry. I only had myself to blame for the shrill anger that was being directed towards me. It was no one else's fault but my own.

I still didn't respond in any way at all, because I had no idea what to say in response to her question. I really had no idea what I thought I was doing.

She grabbed me by the shoulder and attempted to pull me off the unconscious girl I was slumped upon. She might have succeeded in dislodging an arm, but the greater part of my body was an immovable dead weight.

The woman with the angry voice was making a scene. I wasn't aware of much at the time, but I was aware of that. She was grappling with me in an increasingly frantic fashion.

People were taking notice. They were stopping their conversations and looking over to see what the woman with the angry voice was so angry about. They were probably finding her increasingly frantic movements quite amusing, because when you've had a drink or two, and you're in the only nightclub in town, you'll find pretty much anything quite amusing.

I suddenly felt very sick indeed, and my nausea threatened to put an abrupt end to my inertia. It threatened to force my hand.

I felt awfully sick. I felt like I was going to be sick. I put my hand over my mouth in a futile attempt to stop whatever was about to come out of it.

Not for the first time that night, I vomited. It went everywhere. There probably wasn't even that much of it, but it still managed to go everywhere. It seemed to have this amazing power to go everywhere.

Sick: all over the worn out black leather sofa, all over the unconscious girl's dress and body, all over myself, and all over the angry woman's shoes and feet.

I inspected the back of my hand; the back of my hand was not a pretty sight. It was covered in sick.

The patrons of the nightclub now formed a definite audience to this unedifying spectacle: some turned away, hands covering their mouths, as if worried that they too might now be sick; others found the spectacle hilarious, as if someone vomiting over themselves, a sofa, an unconscious girl and an angry woman's shoes and feet was the funniest thing they had ever seen. Some just looked on with interest, as they would look on with interest at any unusual thing that was happening.

The angry woman had stopped grappling with me, and was staring down at her shoes and feet in disgust. She was speechless. We had reached an impasse. The unconscious girl remained unconscious, unable to help anyone. I wished I was somewhere else, but to no avail. I wasn't somewhere else; I was where I was.

We might have remained in that wordless state indefinitely had not my old friend, the surly bouncer, at that moment appeared striding purposefully through the crowd of onlookers.

"Right, you little fuck," said the bouncer, addressing me and sounding surlier than ever. "You're coming with me."

He grabbed me with both hands by the collar of whatever I was wearing, being careful to avoid touching the vomit, which was no mean feat, and dragged me off the worn out sofa, and off the unconscious girl.

He tried to pull me to my feet. He wasn't a weak man, but I was a dead weight, and despite his best efforts, I fell in a useless heap on the floor.

I imagine that our audience backed away, probably because they were worried that I might vomit again or do something crazy, and they wished to avoid being vomited upon or having something crazy done to them at all costs, which was understandable. I imagine that a clearing formed, and that the bouncer and I were in the middle of it. That's how I imagine it.

I lay there in a heap on the floor, and he was trying to drag me to my feet. I felt like an unwilling participant in a wrestling show, or at least I imagine I did. I can't really remember what I actually felt like at the time, but I can imagine.

"Get up you little shit," the bouncer shouted sternly, like a general in a war movie – or a war, probably – as he kicked me sternly two or three times in the ribs; my precious, fragile and vulnerable ribs; the ribs that I needed to be working properly in order to be any sort of functioning human being.

He kept kicking me. He kicked me eloquently like he really knew what he was doing, like he had kicked a person who lay in a heap on the floor about a thousand times before; like it was, by now, no surprise to find himself kicking a person who lay in a heap on the floor.

I imagine that, had I been an onlooker myself, I might have thought that he made kicking a person who lay in a heap on the ground look remarkably easy. But I'm sure it must be harder than it looks. If you think about it, most things are harder than they look.

After a while, he decided that there was no further advantage to be gained by kicking me while I lay in a heap on the floor. He grabbed me again by the collar of whatever I was wearing. He didn't seem to care anymore about avoiding the vomit smeared all over whatever I was wearing; he probably had vomit all over his hands.

"Stand up, you fucker," he hissed, his face now inches from mine. Saliva sprayed my face and I recoiled from his acrid breath, which made me feel a little nauseous again. But fear settled my stomach.

I tried to stand up, I really did, but whether through drunkenness, fear or shame my limbs were shaking uncontrollably and I couldn't.

The bouncer's patience had run out. He roughly yanked me off the ground, using all the strength at his disposal, which was not an inconsiderable amount of strength, and dragged me out of the nightclub.

If I had been able to distinguish anything distinctly, which I wasn't, I might have noticed my brother looking on contemptuously; and Ratty pointing and laughing and making sure that everyone was paying close attention to my humiliation; and I might also have noticed that The Undertaker remained oblivious, still locked in conversation at the bar. But I didn't distinguish any of these things. I registered nothing but an indistinct blur of sounds, colours and shapes.

The bouncer probably grunted as he dragged me out of the nightclub; the audience probably recoiled and backed off as I passed. The seas probably parted before me.

I could no longer tell if the unconscious girl was still unconscious, or if the angry woman was still angry, though I assumed they were. I wondered if it even mattered anymore and decided that it probably didn't. I had left them behind, in the past.

The front door of the nightclub opened with the sound of rushing air like the sound of a window being opened on an airplane in a movie. It felt as if all the sounds, all the colours, and all the shapes were being sucked out into the street. But, of course, they weren't. That kind of stuff just doesn't happen in real life, even though sometimes it feels like it does.

Once outside the bouncer threw me to the pavement. "Fucking pervert," he said. And then he coughed and spat on the pavement near where I had landed, which was his way of expressing his contempt and disgust. I comforted myself by imagining that the worst was over.

But the worst was not over; not yet. There was still worse to come. There's always worse to come.

I stood up with difficulty, leaning against a wall for support. I was still shaky and wobbled on my feet. I was conscious of nothing more than movement, sound, colour, contempt and disgust.

I staggered, stooping, across the street, wanting to put some distance between myself and the scene of my disgrace, but tripped and fell causing a car to screech to a halt. The driver of the car - who as far as I was concerned was just a blur of movement, sound and colour - was not too happy about it.

"I could have fucking killed you! You fucking idiot! Get out of the fucking road! Fucking hell! Ugh!" said the driver of the car.

I can understand why he was angry. After all, he could have killed me and then he would've had to live with my death on his conscience. That was why he was angry. No one in their right mind wants someone else's death on their conscience. That is probably the last thing that someone in their right mind wants on their conscience, or anywhere near their conscience for that matter. And you can understand why. I couldn't blame the guy for being angry. I had no one but myself to blame. Not the surly bouncer, or the angry woman, or the unconscious girl, or Ratty, or The Undertaker, or my brother, or anyone else for that matter. I only had myself to blame.

People were probably looking at me: the guy who had caused all the trouble. One or two probably thought to themselves that it would have better for everyone - apart from the driver of the car, of course - if I had been killed. The surly bouncer probably shook his head sternly, registering his disapproval for all to see, or maybe he had gone off to wash the vomit off his hands. Either way, his disapproval was implicit, there was no real need for him to register it for all to see.

I crawled to the kerb on the other side of the street, and slumped in the doorway of a furniture shop. I sat there and caught my breath.

I closed my eyes, which was just about the only thing I was capable of doing, and it wasn't long before I passed out, which was the only other thing I was capable of doing.

I was spent. I had nothing left to give. Or take.

The Next Thing I Knew

The next thing I knew someone was pouring some sort of spirit over my head. It was my brother. He was laughing maniacally, like a maniac. His friends laughed along with him as if humiliating a person not in their right mind was the funniest thing that anyone could do.

I rose to my feet, coughing and spluttering, and in a desperate fury blindly lashed out in as many directions as I could.

"Stop it! Fuck off! Leave me alone!" I screamed desperately, but that only made them laugh harder. My desperation amused them. They were doubled up. There was at least two of everyone.

I blinked and wiped my stinging eyes; I shook myself like a wet dog. People were staring at me; I was the kind of thing that people stared at.

And that's it. I can't honestly say that I remember anything else that happened that night. The next thing I remember is waking up the next morning on the roof of the boat, and having no idea how I'd got there. No idea at all.

When I woke up on the roof of the boat, the roof of the boat wasn't in the perfectly ordinary market town anymore; the roof of the boat was surrounded by fields and blue and fresh air, and I had no idea how it had got there.

Picture the Scene

Picture the scene:
It's midsummer.

A river wanders lazily through the countryside, its motion so unhurried that it almost appears not to be moving at all, but you know it is because that is what rivers do.

Rivers flow. They can't help it. They don't have any choice. That's what they do and you just have to accept it. Rivers flowing is beyond your control.

Ducks float indifferently on its surface, turning left or right as if following invisible paths, as if for some unknown reason they absolutely have to turn left or right at that exact moment.

Flying insects hover busily in swarms as if they know something that no other living creature knows. And who are you to say that they don't? No one, that's who. You are no one to say that they don't know something that no other living creature knows. And, in fact, the more you think about it, the more likely it seems that they do know something that no other living creature knows. Why wouldn't they? Surely every living creature knows at least one thing that no other living creature knows.

Are you still picturing the scene? Picture it. Imagine that you're there, walking along the riverbank.

The water is murky, like something else that is murky, and you can't see beyond its surface. The surface of the water reflects the air and whatever else that hangs above it.

Vegetation grows in abundance all around the river. Reeds guard the riverbank. If there had been even a slight breeze the reeds might have swayed gracefully in the slight breeze, but there isn't even a slight breeze and the reeds don't appear to be moving at all.

Trees hang protectively over the water, casting shadows that make the water appear black and soundless, and where the shadows fall the water appears to be of infinite depth, or of no depth at all.

If you look closely you might notice small intricate birds surveying the countryside imperiously. If they notice you looking closely at them they will fly away quickly as if they can't believe the gall of you. Looking at them closely? Indeed! How dare you?

Beyond the river and the vegetation that surrounds it, you can see green fields stretching away into the distance. The fields are neatly arranged into rectangles and divided by hedgerows because human beings decided a long time ago that fields couldn't simply be left to their own devices.

It's midsummer.

It's shortly after dawn and the sun is peeking at you from a long way away; its light touches everything you can see and though the light is not the brightest, it is the most revealing. Everything is discovered in its purest form. It is an honest kind of light. It's the kind of light that nothing can hide from.

It's midsummer so it is fairly warm. You don't really need a jumper or a coat, so you left your jumper or coat at home or on the back seat of your car. It's fairly warm, but there is a slight chill in the air nonetheless, as you would expect. Remember: it's shortly after dawn, and even in midsummer, and even on very hot days, dawn is accompanied by a slight chill, because that is just how these things work. It is a dawn chill, and it's to be expected.

There is a slight chill in the air, but you find it quite pleasant because it is midsummer and you know it will soon be rather warm and there will no longer be a slight chill in the air. And when the chill is gone you will miss the slight chill. You are aware of this and so you don't begrudge the slight chill in the air.

It's going to be a fine day. The sky is clear with only a few fluffy white clouds wandering aimlessly across it. One or two of these clouds are reflected in the lazy, murky water below.

Imagine that. Picture it.

The air smells clean and fresh as if it's just got out of the shower, or just had a bath.

A path follows the river. It's not made of gravel, or concrete, or asphalt. Those things would not fit with the scene. It's made of dirt. It is a light brown colour. It is the light brown colour of deliberate, well-trodden dirt that reminds you of your childhood.

It's shortly after dawn and there is no one walking along the path. Apart from the occasional quack of a duck or the occasional chirp of a bird, it is perfectly quiet and still.

There is no distant roar of traffic, or distant growl of an airplane overhead; nor are there any boats drifting up or down the river. Those things have not yet begun to happen because it is still very early in the day and those things will not start to happen until a bit later in the day.

And besides, the scene you are picturing does not exist for those things, for the traffic and the airplanes and the boats, it exists for the other things, the ducks and the reeds and insects and the trees and the reflections of trees and the dirt path. It exists for things that don't make a lot of noise.

A wispy mist clings to the ground as if a cloud fell from the sky. It doesn't make any noise at all.

It's midsummer. It's shortly after dawn and no one's about. Just you. And that's about it. There's not really anything else, apart from, perhaps, a church spire pointing at the sky in the distance; or maybe a bit of processed wood, a panel from a fence perhaps, floating thoughtlessly on the surface of the water.

You might also spot the odd piece of rubbish – an empty can or crisp packet or maybe a plastic bottle of some description. And the rubbish might irritate you a little. You might wonder how the rubbish got there and what sort of person would dump their rubbish in such a beautiful place.

Picture the scene:
It's midsummer.
A river wanders lazily.
It's shortly after dawn.
There's no one about.

You might spot the odd piece of rubbish, but whether you do or not, and if you do what kind of rubbish you spot, is up to you. But if you do spot the odd piece of rubbish, then the odd piece of rubbish represents reality, whatever that is. It is a symbol: a clumsy, unnecessary, irritating symbol.

Along the riverbank there are two or three barges moored at some distance from each other. There is no need for the barges to clump together; there is plenty of room. The barges keep their distance from each other. They are not seeking company; they are seeking peace and quiet, and they have found it. Everything here makes hardly any noise at all, or absolutely no noise whatsoever. It is peaceful, and quiet.

You walk along the riverbank. You round a bend. You walk past the two or three barges that are keeping their distance from each other.

In the distance you see another boat, which you hadn't been able to see before rounding the bend. There are no other boats nearby.

You are surprised to see two men talking conspiratorially at the bow of the boat, or it might be the stern because you have never been able to remember which is which, despite being told a number of times. You are surprised because there is no one else about, and you hadn't expected to see anyone else about, let alone two men talking conspiratorially.

One of the men is tall and thin, while the other is short and fat, because that is just the way things work. If one man is tall and thin then the other man is usually short and fat, so as to form a contrast. I don't know why it is necessary to form a contrast, and nor do you – or maybe you do - but like I say, that is just the way things work.

We are both grown-ups and so we accept that this is just the way things work. It is beyond our control, and so we have no choice but to accept it.

While the two men talk conspiratorially, you notice another man sleeping on the roof of the same boat. The man is sleeping in such an awkward and unnatural position that you can't help wondering if he'll ever wake up.

That man is me, if you hadn't guessed that already.

You can't help but think that this is all very strange.

'This is all very strange,' you think to yourself.

You carry on walking along the riverbank, as if you are stalking the river, as if you are following it to see where it could possibly be going at this unearthly hour, trying to absorb yourself in the natural beauty all around you. But your attention is involuntarily drawn to the two men talking conspiratorially at the bow, or stern, of the boat that you are slowly nearing. You can't help but feel that they are up to no good.

'What good could they possibly be up to?' you can't help but wonder.

'And why is that man sleeping on the roof of the boat in such an awkward and unnatural position? Maybe he's dead,' you think to yourself. 'What the hell is going on here?'

You can't help but wonder what the hell is going on. It's beyond your control. You have been programmed to wonder what the hell is going on whenever it is not entirely clear what the hell is going on.

You slow down so you can observe the scene for as long as possible, without making it obvious that you are doing any such thing. You want to observe the scene for as long as possible, but you do not wish the two conspiratorial men, who you suspect are up to no good, to think that you are watching them. If you know one thing about conspiratorial men, which you do, it is that they do not like the thought of other people watching them.

So you walk slowly along the riverbank, as if simply enjoying the natural beauty that surrounds you, while watching the boat and the two conspiratorial men (Ratty and The Undertaker) and the sleeping man (me) out of the corner of your eye.

Your caution is understandable. The scene looks suspicious. There is definitely something not quite right about it. Naturally, you wish to avoid coming to any harm, or putting yourself in a potentially dangerous situation. This is not cowardice; it is common sense.

Out of the corner of your eye you think you can see the two conspiratorial men laughing, and this impression is confirmed when you hear, a fraction of a moment later, the sound of laughter floating through the air, carried further than seems possible in the profound stillness and quietness of the hour.

It is midsummer and the air is already starting to warm. The slight chill in the air is disappearing and you are glad that you left your jumper or coat at home, or on the back seat of your car.

You carry on walking as slowly as you can, stealing glances of the boat and its occupants while gazing all around you at the trees, the river and whatever patches of blue and green you can see from where you are. You are pretending to be absorbed in contemplation of the majesty of nature, which is a perfectly reasonable thing to be absorbed by when it is midsummer and shortly after dawn, and you are walking slowly along a riverbank.

You notice movement out of the corner of your eye and steal a glance in the direction of the boat.

You see the short fat man pull himself with difficulty onto the roof of the boat. He stands on the roof unsteadily and steadies himself. He steadies himself by placing his feet wide apart and putting his arms out to his sides. Steadied, he offers the tall thin man his hand, but the tall thin man dismisses his offer and pulls himself onto the roof of the boat with an easy fluid motion.

The two men exchange a brief conspiratorial whisper, and then start walking slowly along the roof of the boat. The short fat man walks cautiously with his arms out at his sides as if he is walking along a tightrope; the tall thin man walks casually with his hands in his pockets, as if trying to form as much of a contrast with his companion as possible.

You take several quick steps forward. Your curiosity is getting the better of you and you want to take a closer look. You do, however, take pains to ensure that you are not noticed. You tread lightly and take advantage of whatever cover the riverbank provides.

As you draw nearer you begin to observe the details of the scene: the short fat man's fleshy jowls; the tall thin man's sunken eyes; the sleeping man's bloodstained clothes and hands.

The sight of the blood appals you. It makes you feel a bit wobbly; perhaps your empty stomach begins to feel a little unsettled. You worry that you might be sick, which would blow your cover, as you are incapable of vomiting quietly. But you take a few deep breaths and decide that you will be fine.

You wonder whether it would not be best to turn around and run off through the adjacent field, or hide in a bush, or just go back the way you came.

'But,' you reason, 'humanity didn't get where it is today by running off through the adjacent field, or hiding in a bush, or just going back the way it came.'

You resolve to carry on observing the scene, even though you have no idea what the hell is going on and you suspect that the two conspiratorial men are up to no good. You are not unaware that you are potentially putting yourself in a situation of personal danger. You suspect yourself of bravery.

You observe the two men, shielded by vegetation, talking quietly over the prone body of the unconscious man – me.

You know that I'm sleeping now, rather than dead as you had previously suspected, because you can see my trunk rising and falling as I breathe. You are close enough to see my trunk rising and falling as I breathe, however close that is. Pretty close, I should think.

You are reasonably sure that the two conspiratorial men standing over my prone body haven't noticed you, but you are taking no chances. You are probably not the sort of person who takes unnecessary or foolish risks.

Only unnecessary or foolish people take unnecessary or foolish risks.

You crouch down as if you are investigating something of particular interest on the ground, a colony of ants perhaps, or an unusual flower, but you are not investigating something of particular interest on the ground; you are crouching down because you are close enough to see my trunk rising and falling as I breathe, and though you are reasonably sure that the two conspiratorial men haven't noticed you, you are taking no chances.

You are obscured by vegetation and you can observe without being seen yourself. In your nervous and excited state, your breathing is shallow and fast; it is almost out of control. You try to calm it down but you can't. Your mouth feels dry. You lick your lips, but it doesn't really help.

You look around. There is no one else about, apart from you and the three men on the boat. You stare intently at the unfolding drama in front of you.

You are close enough to hear the voices of the two men talking conspiratorially over the prone slumbering body. You listen intently, but all you can hear is an indistinct mumble and you are not able to make out a single word of what they are saying.

You are still breathing heavily, in quick shallow breaths, as you watch, through the undergrowth, the two conspiratorial men crouch by the sleeping man's body.

The short fat man reaches out a hand and places it on the sleeping man's shoulder; he then shakes the sleeping man, as if testing how much force will be necessary to rouse him gradually from his slumber, and you watch him do so. The sleeping man does not respond in any way to being shaken. The two men exchange a look and perhaps a few whispered conspiratorial words.

The short fat man starts shaking the sleeping man again, but harder this time.

Still there is no response from the sleeping man.

'Maybe he really is dead,' you think to yourself. 'But no,' you reason, 'I can see his trunk rising and falling, he can't possibly be dead.'

The short fat man starts shaking the sleeping man again, but even more violently this time.

The sleeping man wakes with a start.

You watch as he sits up with a jolt and looks around wildly, as if he was having a bad dream, and suspects that it has followed him to reality.

You watch the no longer sleeping man as he waves his arms in front of his face, like he is trying to protect himself from a bad dream, which may well be exactly what he is doing.

Your knees begin to ache from crouching down for so long, but that doesn't stop you noticing the two conspiratorial men exchange a bemused look.

You feel an overwhelming desire to get as far away as possible as quickly as possible. Whatever is going on here you don't like the looks of it. You suddenly feel that this is something that you shouldn't be watching. Your curiosity has satisfied its appetite.

You decide to walk on. You have thought it all through and you consider that to be the safest option. You decide to continue on your way and walk briskly past the boat, as if nothing out of the ordinary is happening at all.

'Maybe,' you think hopefully to yourself, 'nothing out of the ordinary is happening at all.'

You stand up. Your legs are shaky. You start walking towards the boat. As if nothing out of the ordinary is happening at all.

How I Remember it

The first thing I knew was that I had opened my eyes. And, for a moment, that was all I knew. All that I knew was that I had opened my eyes. Nothing else. For a moment.

The next thing I knew was the face of Ratty, hovering above me.

"He's awake," said Ratty, as if it was a matter of grave importance.

His words were directed at The Undertaker who also hovered above me. Their faces loomed above me.

The Undertaker looked at me as if I was a thing of some interest for one reason or another. "Are you all right, mate?" he said.

I couldn't reply. My head felt unusual, as if there was something inside it that didn't want to be there. I tried to remember something, but my head only filled with vague feelings of shame and regret.

I was filled with the knowledge that I had done something shameful, but I had no idea what.

'Where am I?' I thought, once I realised that I had no idea where I was.

I looked around frantically trying to determine where I was, but no amount of frantic looking around helped me to determine where I was. All I knew was that I was somewhere I had no recollection of ever having been before.

"Where am I?" I said.

Neither Ratty nor The Undertaker, who were both looking down at me with grave expressions, thought fit to answer.

My whole body felt sore and the early morning light was blinding. But the early morning light wasn't really blinding at all, it just felt like it was.

My head was throbbing and the early morning light wasn't helping, so I shut my eyes as tightly as I could and buried my head in my arms.

At that moment I had a sensation of something rushing towards me, and I flung my arms in front of my face in a desperate attempt to defend myself. But there was nothing rushing towards me, and I thought I was going mad. In that moment, I thought that was it for me. I gave myself up as mad.

'I'm mad,' I thought. 'That's it for me. Something has happened and now I've gone mad.'

I thought that I'd woken up in a horrible nightmare.

I writhed around on the roof of the boat, moaning and whimpering. Ratty was trying to hold me down, but he wasn't having much luck. I waved my arms in the air and threw myself about, as if waving my arms in the air and throwing myself about was my only hope.

I might have screamed out. My mind was so disordered that I couldn't tell you whether I screamed out or not, or whether the fit lasted for a few seconds or a few minutes.

Ultimately The Undertaker was called upon to restrain me, which he did roughly. "Right, you need to calm the fuck down, mate," he said, calmly but firmly. It seemed to work. I calmed down.

You just don't argue with a guy who buries people for a living. Believe me, you just do what he says.

I looked up at the blue sky, and the few fluffy white clouds that wandered lazily across it, through half-closed eyes. The sky looked familiar, yet also different somehow. It was as if I had noticed something about it that I had never noticed before, though I wasn't sure what it was.

I could hear footsteps approaching. Your footsteps. You were getting closer and closer. I couldn't see you because I was lying down and couldn't turn my head because it hurt too much, but you got closer and closer regardless.

The fact that I couldn't see you because I was lying down and I couldn't turn my head because it hurt too much seemed to have no bearing on your movements whatsoever. You carried on getting closer regardless.

You must have been getting very close indeed or I wouldn't have been able to hear your footsteps.

I couldn't see you myself, but through my half-closed eyes I could see that The Undertaker was watching you. His expression changed from grave to amiable, and I guessed that you and he had made eye contact. The Undertaker was the kind of person who could change his expression in an instant to suit the situation. He was that kind of person. The Undertaker was a master of insincerity.

"Morning," he said, in your direction, as if there was nothing out of the ordinary happening at all. "Too much to drink," he said, as you walked by, as if that explained everything.

If you hadn't been observing the strange scene already, you would doubtless have assumed that this was a man with absolutely nothing to hide, and that nothing out of the ordinary was happening at all. Perhaps you managed to convince yourself that nothing out of the ordinary was happening after all.

You didn't answer verbally, perhaps you were worried that your voice would falter or perhaps you just couldn't think of anything to say, but I imagine that you raised your hand or nodded in The Undertaker's general direction in acknowledgement of his amiable greeting. It would have been rude not to and you're certainly not rude. You may be many things, but being rude is definitely not one of them.

Whatever the case, you didn't answer The Undertaker's greeting verbally but passed mutely on by. You definitely didn't want to get drawn into a conversation. But no doubt you took as good a look at me as you dared, and noted again the bloodstains on my hands and clothes; no doubt you wondered what events could possibly have led to me lying on the roof of a boat with bloodstains on my hands and clothes. And no one would have blamed you for doing so. Your curiosity is entirely within reasonable bounds.

The Undertaker watched you carefully for a minute or so until you were out of sight. When you had disappeared from view he turned back to me. The grave expression had returned. Ratty wore one also. Neither man spoke for a moment, so I tried to.

"Wh-?"

I tried to ask where I was again, but I couldn't speak because I needed to clear my throat. I cleared my throat with a little cough. Ahem.

"Where am I?" I asked in a cracked and broken voice.

"That's not important right now," said The Undertaker. "Listen mate, do you remember anything about last night?"

I tried to remember something about the previous night, beyond the feelings of shame and regret, which I was filled with. And I did remember things about the previous night. It was coming back to me.

I remembered the restaurant and the oriental crackers and the nearest pub and the other people's drinks and the line and the nightclub and the whisky and the unconscious girl and the angry woman and the bouncer and the pavement and the doorway of the furniture shop. As you know

I remembered all of those things – even though I had no wish to – and they explained the feelings of shame and regret that I was filled with. I winced, remembering my shame, and I knew even then that I had no one to blame but myself.

"No," I lied, in reply to The Undertaker's question. I'm not sure if it was habit or shame that made me lie, but either way it was a lie.

I am a practised liar. It comes naturally to me.

"That's probably a good thing," said Ratty, exchanging a meaningful look with The Undertaker, who spoke next.

"Listen mate," he said. "There's no easy way to say this." He looked around, as if checking to see whether anyone was listening. "You fucking killed someone last night."

There was a pause. A momentary silence while The Undertaker let this information sink in.

'You fucking killed someone last night,' I thought, repeating the words in my head, but it made no sense at all. It couldn't possibly be true. I frantically tried to remember what had happened after the doorway of the furniture shop, but I couldn't. There was nothing there. Only darkness. Nothingness.

"What?" I said, in a pathetic attempt to make some sort of sense of it all.

The grave expressions of the two men above me were like clouds that threatened rain.

"He said, you killed a man last night," said Ratty, like an echo of his more solemn friend.

'He said, you killed a man last night,' I thought, but still it made no sense at all. I wondered how I could make it make sense, but there didn't seem to be any way.

"How?" I said, in a desperate attempt to make some sort of sense of it all.

"Look at your hands," said The Undertaker, as if revealing delicate information.

I looked at my hands. The skin was sore and grazed, and they were covered in dried blood and dirt; dried blood was wedged deep within the crevices of my fingernails, as if it was trying to remind me of something.

There was no way of knowing whose blood had dried deep within the crevices of my fingernails, or what it was trying to remind me of.

"Look at your fucking clothes, mate."

I looked at my fucking clothes. My fucking clothes were covered in patches of dried blood and dirt. In one or two places they were ripped and torn.

I sank a little, within myself, as if a little corner of killing someone last night had started to make some sort of sense.

"Look at your face."

The Undertaker handed me a pair of mirrored sunglasses, which had been hooked in his shirt pocket. I examined a reflection of my face. I could see a purpling bruise on one side of my face. I used my hand to touch it. It was painfully sore. I sank a little more, within myself, and the little corner of some sort of sense began to spread.

It was spreading quickly. Killing someone last night was starting to make some sort of sense.

I have never considered myself a good person, which made it easier to believe I had killed someone the previous night.

'Maybe, it's true,' I thought. 'Maybe I did kill someone last night.' I had never truly thought such things entirely beyond me. I had no idea what I was actually capable of.

My eyes opened a little wider; the light no longer felt quite so blinding. "How?" I said. "What happened?"

"You beat a guy to death with a fucking rock, that's how, you fucking psycho," said Ratty, who lacked his friend's professional tact.

"But why?" I said.

"Well, mate," said The Undertaker, continuing his little piece of life-changing oratory with a grave expression. "We were walking through the park on our way back to the boat. You were wasted, and you started shouting abuse at this guy and his girlfriend. He was a fucking soldier, mate. I don't know what you were thinking. There was no way he was going to take that shit. You were pretty foul, mate, I have to say. He punched you in the face, a couple of times. You fell to the ground. I thought he'd knocked you out, mate.

"His girlfriend ran off and he started kicking you in the ribs. He started really kicking the shit out of you." I felt my ribs. They were, indeed, sore. Evidence. Reality gave weight to his words. "He was in a fucking rage. We tried to get him to stop but he wouldn't take any notice. It was just the three of us; we'd lost the rest of them. Anyway, eventually he wore himself out. He stood there panting for a moment, spat on you as you lay on the ground, and walked off. But then, well, I've never seen anything like it before. You fucking lost it, mate."

"You're a fucking psycho," said Ratty, but no one paid him any attention.

The Undertaker continued: "You staggered to your feet, felt around in the dirt for a few seconds and picked up a rock. You raised the rock up above your head and started screaming like a fucking maniac. He barely had time to turn around before you brought the rock crashing down on his skull. There was a cracking sound. He fell to the ground and you beat the poor fucker to death. You smashed his head in. You beat him to a fucking pulp."

The Undertaker spoke quietly but intensely and his words carried weight. He was a man it was hard to doubt, or at least he was a man I found it hard to doubt at the time. It's hard to doubt a man who disposes of the dead for a living. Disposing of the dead gives a man gravitas.

'He is telling me the truth,' I thought. 'I killed a man last night.'

"You dragged the body into a bush and covered it with leaves and dirt," said The Undertaker.

I looked at my hands and knees; they were dirty. Dirt was wedged beneath my fingernails. And blood. Proof. Evidence. Sense.

"You were virtually catatonic after that, mate. We had to carry you back to the boat. You came to for a moment when we got back. You wouldn't go inside. You climbed up here and passed out." The Undertaker paused. He took a deep breath, then exhaled, as if it had all been quite an ordeal for him. "We heard sirens so we thought we'd better get the hell out of there at the first opportunity. We set off just before dawn, and here we are. You should be safe here for a while."

The Undertaker said all this so quietly and intensely, and with such grave solemnity, fitting for the occasion, that I believed every word.

There was a sudden noise from the nearby shrubbery. My heart was palpitating. The Undertaker froze dramatically. But it was only a bird, or some other kind of small animal, doing exactly what birds, or some other kind of small animal, are expected to do.

"What am I going to do?" I said, pathetically.

The Undertaker sighed regretfully. "For starters," he said, "stay out of sight for the rest of the weekend. Say you're not feeling well." He looked around as if anyone could be watching. "And don't ever tell anyone anything about what happened. Especially not your brother. He'd go fucking mental." He paused. "You can't trust anyone with shit like this, mate." He looked at Ratty then back at me. "We three are the only ones that ever need know about this. Understood?" I nodded. Ratty nodded. It was almost like we were in it together, but of course we weren't.

I was in it on my own.

I had this funny feeling for a moment that I was half-sitting, half-lying in a room of infinite size; of such infinite size that its walls could hardly be seen. The room was the enormity of what I had done.

I looked out across the river. The world looked different because I was a murderer. Everything was remarkably still as if waiting for an opportunity to betray me. Suddenly, the world seemed somehow duplicitous. I watched a bird fly from its perch and melt into the air, and I imagined it treacherously carrying news of the murder far and wide.

'What the hell am I going to do?' I thought. And I had absolutely no answers at all. None whatsoever.

That is how I remember it.

Taking the Undertaker's Advice

I spent a miserable day trapped inside the boat haunted by blurred images and shards of memory from the previous night, which were busily arranging themselves in accordance with The Undertaker's narrative.

I slept for most of the day. I stayed inside the boat and slept fitfully. But I didn't dream. I didn't have a single dream. And you know how people say that you always have loads of dreams when you sleep you just don't remember them? Well, I didn't have any dreams; I didn't have a single dream that I remembered or otherwise. And I know that for a fact, even though there's no way I could possibly know that for a fact.

I slept fitfully, and whenever I woke up I immediately closed my eyes and tried to return to sleep, before I started thinking about beating a man to death with a rock the night before. Most people will never know what it feels like to think that they've beaten a man to death with a rock the night before, but it doesn't feel too great, let me tell you, not too great at all.

One time I woke up and couldn't get back to sleep. I could hear my brother outside talking to The Undertaker. It just so happened that he was talking about me.

"What the fuck's he doing down there?" said my brother.

"I think he overdid it a bit last night, mate," said The Undertaker.

"I really don't know why I fucking invited him," said my brother.

"No," said The Undertaker, distantly, probably thinking about something else. "He's not much fun."

"Not much fun?" said my brother, as if he couldn't possibly let his friend get away with such gross understatement. "He's a walking fucking funeral."

The Undertaker sighed, probably thinking about one or two of the many funerals he had attended as part of his professional duties. "You're not wrong," he said. He wasn't going to argue; he wasn't going to stick up for me, and I had no reason to expect him to.

He came to see me later. The Undertaker. Not my brother. My brother didn't come to see me at all.

"How are you feeling?" he asked.

"Um," I said. I didn't know what to say. I had no words to describe how I was feeling.

"Don't worry, your brother doesn't suspect a thing," said The Undertaker, as if that made everything all right, which it didn't.

"Oh," I said, and it was all I could think of to say. I couldn't think of anything to say beyond inarticulate, monosyllabic sounds, which meant nothing.

"Look, it will be all right," said The Undertaker, and I believed him. He was a man I just instinctively believed. I trusted him. I felt a little reassured.

"OK," I said, which was a slight improvement on my previous utterance.

'He disposes of the dead,' I thought. 'What he says must be true. He must know what he's talking about.'

I was lying on one of the boat's bunks as he spoke to me, and The Undertaker seemed to tower above me, but I didn't feel vulnerable. I felt like he was protecting me, like he had my best interests at heart. I should have known that my impression of him had nothing to do with the truth. I should have known. Looking back, it seems obvious.

I was a fool, but it's easy to say that now.

"You've just got to lie low for a while. It'll blow over. You'll be fine. Just try not to draw too much attention to yourself."

"OK," I said, almost hopefully. I thought I would be good at not drawing attention to myself.

"Right, well, we're going out for a few drinks now. You're welcome to come, but I think it would be best if you stay here tonight. Lie low. You don't want someone recognising you or anything. Just get some rest. You'll feel better for it. I'll tell them you're still not feeling well."

There was a moment where neither of us spoke.

"Will you let me know if you hear anything?" I said. I had to ask. I needed to know.

"About what, mate?" said The Undertaker, as if he didn't know.

"About the …" I trailed off. I couldn't say it.

The Undertaker got my meaning. "Oh, of course. Of course, I will, it's the least I can do."

But it wasn't the least he could have done. He could have told me the truth then and there. He could have told me the truth then and there and everything would have been all right. But he didn't. He didn't tell me the truth then and there, and everything wasn't all right.

He's only got himself to blame.

We've all only got ourselves to blame.

"See you later then, mate," said The Undertaker.

"See you later," I said, and he was gone.

The Warehouse Industry

I lay there alone in the dusky stillness, and listened to the laughter of my brother and his friends as they disappeared into the night.

When I Got Home

When I got home, I couldn't find my keys, so I knocked on the door.

"Knock, knock, knock," said my hand, as it knocked on the wooden door. At least I think it was wooden. It may have been pretending to be wooden. That's what some things do nowadays: they pretend to be something that they're not. Don't ask me why.

I've never really understood why things are the way they are. The world is still a mystery to me.

The girl I used to live with when I worked at the pie factory answered the door. Except I didn't yet work at the pie factory, so she was just the girl I used to live with.

"Oh, you're back," said the girl I used to live with. "Nice of you to let me know," she added, sarcastically.

I was pretty sure I had told her when I was going to be back, but maybe I hadn't. I certainly hadn't spoken to her while I was away.

"Hello," I said, trying to sound cheerful. However, despite my best efforts, it was still a pretty rotten attempt.

"Yes. 'Hello'. That was implied," said the girl I used to live with.

"Can I come in?" I said.

"Well, you live here, don't you?" said the girl I used to live with.

"Yes," I said.

"Well, you better come in, then," said the girl I used to live with, and she moved aside to let me through. I guess that was the kind of person she was; I guess she was the kind of person who never sounded too pleased to see you. But I can't be too sure. I never really got to know her all that well.

I took The Undertaker's advice. The next day I stayed at home and tried not to draw attention to myself. It turned out I was right: I was good at it. It came naturally to me.

It was late when the girl I lived with returned home from work. She worked as a barmaid at a nearby pub. You'll remember, I'm sure, that we once tried unsuccessfully to have sex behind a skip in the car park. That had already happened, and we never tried again.

She took one look at me, and curled her lip in evident distaste. "You should get a job," she told me.

I didn't reply.

"Did you hear me?" she said. "You should get a job."

"What kind of job?" I said, and it was a genuine question. I had no idea what kind of job I should get, and I had no idea what kind of job I would be able to do. But I had no money, and nothing to do, so she was right: I needed to get a job.

If there's one thing you need, and there is, it's money. And something to do as well, probably.

"The pie factory are always looking," said the girl I used to live with. "They're always looking for people and they don't ask too many questions. You'll be able to get a job there without too much fuss."

'And without drawing too much attention to myself,' I thought.

And once I had the job, I guessed that no one would pay too much attention to a guy that works in a pie factory.

'The pie factory it is then,' I thought to myself.
And the pie factory it was.
You remember the pie factory, don't you?

It was a relief to finally leave the country house where my brother's second wedding reception was being held. I'd had more than enough; more than more than enough, if that's even possible.

It had been an immense effort to last as long as I did and I doubt I could have lasted a second longer. I think I would have screamed, or wept, or collapsed, or something. I thought that I'd done pretty well to last as long as I did. I was almost proud of myself, which was an odd, unfamiliar feeling.

I walked outside into the fresh air of a fine spring day. At least I think it was a fine spring day. Certainly, when I remember walking outside into the fresh air, it is the fresh air of a fine spring day, but whether it actually was or not I can't be too sure.

I'm never too sure about most things, but you probably know that by now.

The air was fresh and tasted like some sort of freedom. I wouldn't say I felt hopeful, but I felt relieved, which is a pretty good substitute if hopefulness is beyond reach, which it was.

The din of chatter faded behind me, which was exactly what I wanted it to do, and it was a huge relief to hear the din of chatter fading behind me.

There was a solitary man standing outside the house smoking a cigarette. He looked at me strangely like he wanted to say something, but wasn't sure whether he ought to or not. Thankfully he decided not to. I definitely didn't want him to say anything to me. As far as I was concerned, the man made the right decision.

I tried to pretend that I knew exactly what I was doing, but of course I didn't. Of course, I had absolutely no idea what I was doing. I was living from one moment to the next, as I have always done, without giving much thought to anything else.

I headed towards the prettily manicured gardens, which stretched out in front of the house on either side of a perfectly straight, tree-lined, asphalt - at least I think it was asphalt - drive. You know the kind of drive I mean: the kind of drive that old country houses usually have.

I'm pretty sure that the man who was standing outside the house smoking a cigarette watched me until I had disappeared behind some shrubbery, and he couldn't see me anymore. I can't be certain, but I'm pretty sure. I wasn't what you would expect from a wedding guest, so I was probably a thing to be watched, especially if, as was the case, there was nothing else to be watched.

I cursed myself for coming. After all these years of successfully not drawing attention to myself, I had let myself down. I had put myself in a situation where not drawing attention to myself was almost impossible.

After a few minutes of walking around the prettily manicured gardens, and making sure that I could not be seen by the man who was smoking a cigarette outside the house, or anyone else who might be smoking a cigarette, or doing anything else outside the house, I decided to lie down behind a prettily manicured shrub. I was exhausted from the day's trials and so lying down behind a shrub seemed like a good idea. I needed a rest.

I lay down on the grass. The grass was amazing. It was soft and buoyant. It was neither too long nor too short. It was just the right length. It was fragrant as well, but not too fragrant. It was just the right amount of fragrant. It felt like it had been well looked after. It was amazing grass. I'd never known grass quite like it. Amazing.

I made myself comfortable, and looked up at the blue sky and the little fluffy white clouds that were scattered in front of it. The clouds looked as if they were scattered randomly, but they were probably exactly where they were supposed to be.

I was exhausted, and I felt my eyes closing of their own accord. I quickly fell asleep.

When I awoke it was dark. There was a little chill floating about, or at least there probably was, not that it matters. A little evening chill it was, if there was a chill at all.

As usual I had not dreamt. I had not had a single dream, not even one that I couldn't remember.

I felt like a shell: hollow, hard, and brittle.

I could hear voices in the near distance. They seemed to fall on top of me, like the kind of rain that is a fine mist and covers you in a damp feeling. Everything came to me from above, apart from the sensation of lying on the grass, which no longer felt soft and buoyant; instead it felt cold and flat, like a wet towel.

I could hear a hubbub in the near distance. Occasionally a particularly hearty laugh broke away from the general din, as if trying to make a name for itself, as if trying to draw attention to itself, to the fact of its existence. Listen to me above all others, it seemed to be saying, I am a particularly hearty laugh.

No: focus on the facts.

I was lying on the grass, which was now cold and flat. It was a calm, still night, and there was a little chill floating about. It was spring, or thereabouts.

Above me the sky was clear and I could see a multitude of stars, but they didn't make any sense to me at all, and offered me no comfort whatsoever. They seemed cold, hard and distant, and not designed to offer me any comfort whatsoever.

I could hear voices laughing and talking loudly in the darkness, disturbing the calmness and the clarity of the night. The voices made me feel uneasy. The voices made my whole body feel tense. They made my mind shoot about wildly like a moth crashing into a light outside a country house on a dark spring night. I couldn't make sense of anything. Not the stars, not the voices. Not anything. I closed my eyes, but the voices were still there. Closing my eyes had no effect on the voices at all. The voices couldn't be avoided. They were there and refused to be ignored.

I was a shell. I felt as though I might crack at any moment, because that is what shells do. It's inevitable. At some point, whether it is sooner or later, shells crack. And I was ready to crack. I think I even wanted to crack. I had had enough of not cracking. I think I thought it would be a relief to crack. And relief was my only hope.

'If I crack,' I think I thought, 'I will not be a shell anymore; I will be the broken pieces of a shell, which might be an improvement.' That is what I think I thought. And I think I thought that I needed a change, that any change would be better than more of the same. Don't ask me why. I don't think I had any choice. I don't think I was controlling my thoughts. I think something else was.

I looked straight ahead. Stars kept appearing where before there had only been darkness, and I had no idea why. It made no sense at all. Strange things seemed to be happening which I couldn't account for.

The grass felt cold and flat. I kept focusing on the grass because it was the only thing that seemed to make any sense. It had once been soft and buoyant, but now, because of forces outside of its control, it was cold and flat. That made sense to me. I could understand that.

For some reason, I turned over onto my belly, and pulling myself along the ground, slithered – my stolen suit getting dirtier and dirtier with each passing moment – towards the voices. I think I thought that if I couldn't avoid them, I would have to confront them. I'm not sure why I thought that. Like I said, I was not in control of my thoughts. Something else was.

Excuses, excuses.

Through the bushes that screened me I could see a small crowd of people. Cars drove sporadically along the perfectly straight, tree-lined drive flashing me momentarily with filmic light as they passed. I stopped moving whenever this happened, so as not to draw attention to myself, as anyone who saw me might have thought it a little odd that one of the wedding guests was slithering, in a spasmodic fashion, along the cold damp ground. They might have thought it a little odd, and perhaps a little alarming. Alarm bells might have rung.

Riiinnnnggggg.

Rrrriiiinnnnnnnggggggggg.

Rrrrrriiiiiinnnnnnnnnnnnnnggggggggggggggggggggggg!

I slithered closer; towards the voices, which became louder, as you would expect.

Closer still, for some reason.

Closer.

Clo-ser.

The dirt clung to my stolen clothes, as if trying to make a point.

I could see a crowd of people through the bushes that screened me. I could see them, but they could not see me, which was exactly how I wanted it to be. There was no way I wanted them to be able to see me.

A cinematic flash of light. I stopped moving. It passed.

I slithered closer; towards the voices. Louder and louder still.

The dirt clung to my stolen clothes and was building up beneath my fingernails, as if it was trying to tell me something.

"Hey you," it might have been trying to tell me. "What the fuck do you think you are doing?" Or something like that.

Closer still; until I was close enough to distinguish faces in the crowd: the faces of my brother and his bride; the faces of departing wedding guests saying their goodbyes. Faces to go with the voices. I was close enough to see their mouths move in time with the sounds they were making. That close.

I was close enough to see my brother surrounded by a throng of departing wedding guests. The wedding was over and it was time to say goodbye, so that is what he did: he said goodbye, as expected. He knew what to do and he did it. He was in control of his own thoughts too, which must have helped.

The crowd thinned as my brother performed his duties. And I despised him for performing these duties, and for having had a second wedding, and because it was now time to say goodbye, and because I was slithering along the cold damp ground towards the sound of his voice. I hated him for all of these reasons. Somehow, my hatred for him made sense; like the grass, it made sense. I could understand it.

The crowd gradually thinned exposing the fleshy presence of Ratty and his thin pale companion, standing at my brother's side. They didn't seem to be leaving. They were part of the group being said goodbye to, rather than part of the group saying goodbye.

'They must be staying the night,' I might have thought.

The thin pale woman hugged herself and rubbed her arms as if feeling chilly. It wasn't really cold but there might have been a little chill in the air. She spoke a quiet word in Ratty's ear and disappeared inside the house.

With the thin pale woman gone, The Undertaker appeared at Ratty's side, and the two men laughed loudly at something one or the other said. I could see their mouths moving in time with the sounds they were making. Their laughter pierced the stillness. It was a sour ugly sound like the smell of vinegar.

My brother and his bride were saying goodbye to the last straggling guests. The crowd had thinned itself out of existence. It was no longer a crowd at all.

"Goodbye," said my brother to the last straggling guests. "Thanks for coming."

"Goodbye," said his bride.

"Goodbye," said the last straggling guests. "Thanks for a great day." And I could see their mouths move in time with the sounds they were making. And seeing their mouths move in time with the sounds they were making helped me to make some sort of sense of it all.

Only the four of them now remained.

My brother kissed his bride, and they exchanged a few words and giggled. They looked happy. I almost smiled, despite myself.

"Right," said my brother, who always liked to take control of a conversation, turning to his two friends, "we're going upstairs. We'll see you both in the morning. Good night."

"Good night," said his bride.

"Good night," said Ratty.

"Good night," said The Undertaker. "And remember what I said earlier," he continued, addressing my brother's second wife and winking. "If it doesn't work out, you know where to find me." He winked again. I was close enough to see him winking again.

"You're married, aren't you?" said my brother's second wife, in good humour, playing along. "And you've got a kid, right?"

"Just say the word. I'll dispose of them. I've got contacts." He's an undertaker, remember? He disposes of things for a living.

"Right then," said my brother, regaining control of the conversation. "Good night everyone." He liked to take control of things. He was the kind of person who liked to take control of things. He started walking a step or two behind his bride up the short but grand staircase that led back into the house, but then he turned around, as if he had just remembered something.

"Oh, by the way," he said. "Did you see my brother today?"

"No, I didn't think he was here," said Ratty, looking suddenly disconcerted. The Undertaker just shook his head gravely.

"He was on your table," said my brother, to Ratty. "Didn't you recognise him?"

Ratty thought for a moment. Yes, maybe he did recognise me after all. But he hadn't realised it until now. He hadn't put two and two together. Until now. 'Shit!' he might have thought, putting two and two together.

"Nothing's changed," my brother continued, as no verbal response was forthcoming from either man. "He's still a waste of space."

"Some things never change," said The Undertaker. But he was wrong. Things do change. They change all the time.

"Anyway, good night," said my brother, finally.

"Good night," said Ratty.

"Good night," said The Undertaker.

My brother disappeared inside the house. His bride followed in his wake.

It was just Ratty and The Undertaker left now.

And me: lying on the cold damp ground watching them through a bush that I was hiding behind, for reasons beyond my control.

There was a dramatic flash of light and the sound of a car horn beeping. In response, Ratty and The Undertaker raised their arms and waved. The light passed and disappeared down the perfectly straight tree-lined drive and into the darkness, as if it knew exactly what it was looking for.

Everyone was gone. The coast was clear.

Stillness reasserted itself. I lay dead still. I even tried not to breathe thinking that the sound might give me away, and it might have done too.

You never know what might give you away. Even something as commonplace as the sound of your own breathing can give you away.

I watched the two men: the short fat man and the taller thinner man. It was strange to see them once again, in the flesh, twenty years on. It didn't feel like real life. It felt like a performance of real life. For a moment I doubted whether the two men I was watching had anything to do with me at all. Perhaps I was mistaken. Suddenly I couldn't be sure. Maybe they hadn't really ruined my life after all. Perhaps they weren't who I thought they were. Or perhaps it had all been some sort of misunderstanding. Perhaps I only had myself to blame.

It really is hard to be too certain about things.

Suddenly, I couldn't be too sure about anything.

I could feel myself floating away, and I was determined not to float away. I tried to wrest back some control from whatever something was in control. I anchored myself with certainties: the grass beneath me was certainly cold and damp; the two men were certainly who I thought they were – there was certainly no misunderstanding; and I had every reason to feel nothing but hatred for them. They had ruined me. They had laid waste to me.

They had toyed with my life - something that was of great importance to me and should not have been toyed with.

I watched as The Undertaker took out two cigarettes from the inside pocket of his jacket, and offered one to his shorter fatter companion.

My hatred for the two men tried to slip from my grasp. I reached out and grabbed it, even though it had no physical form. It was a slippery thing all of a sudden.

I concentrated. I didn't want to float away. The grass was cold and damp, and I hated the two men I was watching, who had definitely ruined my life. It was them. It was their fault. The fault lay with them.

My life had been a lie. Or a joke.

I needed to know something true about myself; I needed to believe in something. If that makes any sense at all.

The Warehouse Industry

The two men I hated were talking quietly to each other, so that only an indistinct murmur reached my ears. I watched them smoking calmly, and watched the clouds of smoke that they exhaled, and wondered if I could believe in a cloud of smoke, and thought that, perhaps, if I knew something true about myself, then I could even believe in a cloud of smoke.

I watched the clouds of smoke disappear into the darkness, and desperately wanted to be able to believe in the clouds of smoke, even though they had disappeared and no longer existed.

And I thought that if I knew something true about myself, then perhaps I would be able to believe in things that had disappeared and no longer existed.

I concentrated hard on the hatred I felt towards the two men I was watching so that it didn't float away, like the clouds of smoke and disappear into the darkness.

I searched the ground blindly with my hand, as if I knew exactly what I was looking for. I found what I was looking for. I found a large jagged rock: a large jagged rock that I could just about hold in one hand. I gripped the rock tightly.

It was a cold hard fact. Indisputable. Unarguable. Trustworthy. It was something true that I could believe in.

I imagined that my hatred for the two men I was watching was the large jagged rock that I could just about hold in one hand. I imagined that it wouldn't float away, like the cloud of smoke, and disappear into the darkness. I imagined that it was something that could not be disputed; I imagined that it was unarguable, and could be trusted implicitly.

The two men were smoking, and talking quietly and sporadically to each other. They often remained silent while clouds of smoke floated away and disappeared into the darkness.

Then they would speak again quietly, as if there was really nothing more to say, as if they were only speaking out of habit. There was a sense that everything of moment had already been said.

When they weren't talking quietly to each other, they might have gazed wistfully into the darkness of a fine spring night, or watched the clouds of smoke disappearing into the darkness. They might have. Or they might have just stared at their feet. It was hard to tell in the darkness of a fine spring night, or whatever it was.

It's hard to be certain about details. I've never been too good with details.

I was watching the two men from behind a bush while I gripped a large jagged rock with a white-knuckled hand.

I watched the men and gripped the rock. The two men weren't too far away. I could cover the ground between us in seconds.

If you had been there lying next to me on the cold damp grass, you might have been able to hear a cracking sound; it would have been ever so quiet, but unmistakable.

You know what's going to happen; you've always known what's going to happen. It's inevitable, and it's always been inevitable.

Everything's inevitable. Everything that happens leads to its inevitable consequence. You know that, don't you?

I gripped the large jagged rock - a cold hard fact in the world, an inevitable consequence - with a white-knuckled hand, and slowly rose to my feet. I remained slightly hunched so that I was still screened by the bush I had been hiding behind. I held the large jagged rock firmly in my hand.

The two men were finishing their cigarettes, taking their last inhalation before throwing away their butts.

I rose, unnoticed, to my full height, which was neither considerable nor inconsiderable. I started walking slowly, trying not to draw attention to myself.

The two men turned to go inside. They had not seen me, or heard me, or noticed me whatsoever.

I was pretty good, after all, at not drawing attention to myself. It is the only thing I have ever been much good at.

The Undertaker placed his hand on the shorter fatter man's back as they walked up the short but grand staircase that led back into the house.

I strode towards them, no longer caring whether they noticed me or not, but still they did not notice me.

I gripped the large jagged rock tightly with a white-knuckled hand.

I strode towards the two men. I was so close that there was no way they could not notice me now. I had not given them a choice. They had to notice me. They heard my steps behind them. They turned round. There was a moment of silent recognition, but it was only a moment, and it was over almost as soon as it had begun.

"It's you," said Ratty, his face ashen.

"What the fuck?" said The Undertaker, struggling to understand what was happening.

I didn't reply. I couldn't think of a single thing to say to them. Words failed me. There was nothing I could possibly say, or that there was any need to say.

I didn't stop striding until I was upon them. I raised the rock above my head without hesitation and brought it crashing down on something hard and brittle.

"Fuck!" said Ratty.

"Jesus!" said The Undertaker.

There was the sound of something cracking.

"Crack," said something hard and brittle. It was the sound of Ratty's skull cracking. He fell wordlessly to the ground, because in the end there are no words. In the end, words fail you.

I brought it down again. "Crack!" said Ratty's broken skull. And again and again and again. "Crack! Crack! Crack!"

Each blow was a fact; something true. The truth. Something I could believe in.

The Undertaker, after a moment – but only a moment – of paralysis, tried to run away. I leapt upon him with my rock.

"Crack!" said The Undertaker's skull. He struggled in a futile fashion. "Crack! Crack! Crack!" He had no chance.

And no choice.

For a moment I stood above them: the two men who had once ruined my life, and who I hated, as they died.

'Good,' I might have thought as their lives leaked inevitably from their bodies. 'Good.'

I no longer felt like a shell; I felt like the broken pieces of a shell. It was a relief, which was the best I could have hoped for.

Still gripping the bloodstained rock tightly, I floated away and disappeared into the darkness.

Epilogue

A Happy Ending

The phone rang. I picked it up but didn't say anything. I was feeling miserable because I still had a job.

"Hey cowboy," said the manager's daughter's voice through the wires, attempting to imitate a movie star accent. It was quite embarrassing really. I felt a bit silly. "D'ya wanna fuck?" Her voice was a sultry whisper. "D'ya wanna fuck my tight wet cunt, cowboy?"

I had to admit I did. I was horribly embarrassed and felt terribly silly but I knew the answer was yes; a desperate, pathetic yes, but a yes, nonetheless.

'Maybe this is my reward,' I thought. My reward for staying, for not being made redundant, which was what I had wanted with all my heart.

"Yes," I said truthfully. "I do."

Later that day the manager's daughter strode purposefully into the warehouse. She wore an austere expression on her pretty face, which it looked as though she couldn't wait to discard. She strode purposefully until her austere expression was inches from me, and then she discarded it. It melted away.

Without further preamble, she reached for me and started kissing me passionately, as if she was suddenly, for some reason, unable to control her desire for me any longer, which seemed odd. Her hands squeezed my flesh. Her tongue waggled about in my mouth as if it had lost its keys and was in a hurry.

Then she withdrew with an abrupt movement and looked straight into my eyes. She looked deep within me.

"There's something not quite right about you," she said. But whatever it was, it didn't seem to matter too much.

She started unbuttoning my warehouse trousers. They were the trousers that I always wore at the warehouse. I'm pretty sure I wore the same pair of trousers every single day that I worked at the warehouse. My warehouse trousers.

Still kissing me passionately, she sat on the counter, which was where I practised my craft – my warehouse craft – and pulled up her skirt.

It was a fine spring afternoon; the sun was talking and was interrupted only occasionally by random fluffy clouds, which floated across the sky because that was what they were expected to do.

She wasn't wearing any tights. I caressed her legs feverishly. She grabbed my hand and pulled it towards her crotch. She stroked my private parts.

I wondered if this was what love felt like and decided that it probably was.

A car door slammed somewhere outside of what was happening to me. I heard the car door slam, but it didn't seem relevant, so I ignored it, as if it couldn't possibly have anything to do with me. The sound of the car door was followed by the sound of footsteps, like a shadow. It was as if the sound of footsteps was the sound of the car door's shadow.

The sound of footsteps stopped and was followed by the sight of the manager staring at us in disbelief. It was as if the sight of the manager staring at us in disbelief was the sound of footsteps' shadow.

The manager stared at us in disbelief. He wore paint-stained jeans and a plain black t-shirt. His face was scarlet with rage; an indignant drop of sweat dripped from his hairline across the beaten paths of his forehead.

"What the fuck do you think you're doing?" he said.

A furious globule of saliva flew from his mouth and landed on his daughter's thigh, close to where my hand was resting. He was quite close to us; uncomfortably close. It was all very intimate.

The manager didn't wait for a reply, but grabbed me firmly by the collar. He hurled me with considerable strength into a pile of empty boxes for dramatic effect, which was probably no less than I deserved. I lay there pathetically, surrounded by empty boxes for dramatic effect, my private parts exposed for all to see.

The manager walked over to me menacingly. "I'll teach you to fuck with me! You little shit! You fucking cunt!" he said, and more besides, and each curse was accompanied by a sharp kick to the ribs, or the gut, or the face or the head.

"Oh, for fuck's sake, dad," said the manager's daughter petulantly, as if watching her father kick the shit out of me was a massive inconvenience, as if she had much more important things to be doing.

The manager paused for a moment. "And you can fuck off and all," he said, and then continued administering sharp kicks to the various parts of my body already mentioned. Boxes flew around for dramatic effect. It was all a big drama.

Eventually the manager stopped, exhausted by his rage. His face looked like it might pop, and he was breathing wildly. For a moment, I feared that he might drop dead on top of me, which seemed like a genuine possibility. He reached down and I cowered pathetically, drawing up my legs to shield my vulnerable groin, and covering my face with my hands and forearms.

He reached down and I thought he was going to punch me, but he didn't punch me. Instead, he grabbed me again by the collar, with both hands, and with considerable strength dragged me to my feet.

"Now get the fuck out!" he said, his face inches from mine. His face had never been so close to mine.

It's a funny thing, let me tell you, when someone else's face is so close to your own.

Saliva sprayed in all directions at once and it was no longer possible to notice where the little globules landed.

"Oh, for God's sake," said the manager's daughter, as if tired of it all.

The manager headbutted me and threw me to the floor. It was a stone floor and my landing was painful; there were no empty boxes to cushion my fall or fly around for dramatic effect.

"Get the fuck out," the manager shouted, "and if I ever see your ugly fucking face again …" He made no attempt to finish the sentence. He was panting like an angry dog.

I staggered to my feet and limped out of the warehouse, for the last time.

"Fucking pervert!" said the manager. He ran over to me and kicked my backside. "FUCK OFF!"

I didn't need any encouragement. With one last look behind me, I fucked off.

And as I ran away from the nondescript building and through the nondescript industrial estate in the wholly unremarkable town, a smile spread across my face.

I laughed to myself; I couldn't stop smiling. For some reason I couldn't stop smiling.

It was a fine spring afternoon and, for a moment, for some reason, I was almost happy.

THE END

Printed in Great Britain
by Amazon